Innocent Murderer

by

Jeannette Grindele

This is a work of fiction. Any resemblance of any of the characters to persons living or dead is strictly coincidental.

FIRST EDITION

Library of Congress Catalog Card No: 95-90800
ISBN: 1-56002-618-9

UNIVERSITY EDITIONS, Inc.
59 Oak Lane, Spring Valley
Huntington, West Virginia 25704

Cover by Joyce Dillenberger

Dedication

This book is dedicated to my many friends and family, especially my children who, along the rocky paths of my life, encouraged me to keep on keeping on. A couple of my children encouraged me to buy a computer in order to work faster, when I hardly knew what a computer was. I owe it all to them. Thanks, kids. Thank you all, my friends.

Chapter One

Moving to Atlanta

Leona Lutz paced the floor, then stopped and flung her lipstick-stained cigarette into the overfilled ashtray, a scowl on her line-ridden face. *Where is she anyway? I told her to be here today. If she isn't, I'm ruined!* She reached over and angrily snuffed the cigarette, saying to no one in particular, "The day's nearly gone, and Kutzie Kline hasn't called to let us know if she's in town yet. What if she's changed her mind?"

Bill Davis raised his eyebrows, "It's only 11:00 A.M., Leona. Stop worrying. The salary you're paying her, she'll be here. You have to remember, she's moving here from another state. You're expecting her to get all she needs done in five days, but you need to give her some time."

"How d'ya figure five days?" She dropped her one-hundred-seventy-pound body onto a seat, and licking her fingers, twisted small wisps of dyed-black hair around her fingers, and fretted, "If she doesn't call from somewhere near here before quitting time I'll worry all weekend over whether or not she's changed her mind. She HAS to start work Monday." She pushed away from the desk, sighing deeply. *If Kutzie Kline doesn't look like the photo she sent, I'll kill her, so help me. Only a beautiful woman can handle this job.* Her face revealed the hard woman she was, as she inhaled the smoke deeply into her lungs, and watched it stream from both nostrils. Bill looked at her as if he were waiting for her to answer his question, then went on to say, "Back to how I figure the woman has five days; Didn't you call Miss Kline on the 10th, asking her to start work on the 17th?" He seemed agitated to some extent, with his impatient boss-lady, because many times Leona left a conversation thread hanging in mid-air.

"I did, indeed," the chesty brunette retorted. "What about

it?"

"Well, that gave her only five days if you're expecting her to arrive today. The woman had to pack, move, and find an apartment and move in before Monday. She needed at least through Sunday to get it all done, and start work Monday morning."

"No, no, no! I have to know she's made it to town before we close tonight. I have to know she's in town before the weekend. My hormones can't take this waiting." she barked.

"You know, I just don't understand how you can expect that young, inexperienced girl to do what no one else could." Bill rubbed his chin. "She's never even worked a full-time job before, you said, and you're paying her an unbelievable starting wage to try to work a miracle?"

"Moving to Atlanta from Charlotte, North Carolina is no big deal. She's young. She'd better get everything wrapped up, and come on!"

"That's not what I'm talking about, Leona. The girl has to find a place to live, and get done all that's necessary when one moves, especially to another state. Give her a break!"

"This job must be done. From the way that girl looks in the photo, she can do it, if I know men, that is; and I think I've known enough in my life. Just wait and see, if she doesn't do what she's being hired to do, it's back to Charlotte, North Carolina for her. I'm just tired that Rusty Hunt treats us like nobodies." Bill didn't question the meaning of her last remark, but he looked somewhat fed up with her belly-aching about Kutzie Kline, and the way she was whining already when it was yet early in the day. Evidently he knew she was completely exaggerating the fact that Kutzie's arrival on that particular Friday was of utmost importance, for he changed the subject from why Leona had hired Miss Kline to what she had to accomplish quickly once she arrived in town. "Well, when she does get here I have an apartment lined up for her to see. It's just a block up the street from my place. There's no vacancies where I live, but Chalet Hill Village has a one-bedroom available, and I've been told they're pretty nice. I called the manager on the phone, and she said Miss Kline could move in without all the required checking out a new tenant since I said I'd stand good for her. They have just the one one-bedroom available that's ready to move into. Carpet's cleaned, and it's all been exterminated. She said it usually takes two or three days to check someone's credit, but said they'd waive that procedure."

Leona sniffed, and grunted. *Hush, Bill Davis. All you've done is ramble on about that crap about an apartment. My main concern is getting her here, and she can live in a tent for a week, or a month, or however the hell long she has to, but, WHERE IS SHE NOW?* Aloud, she simply said, "You don't know that Kutzie

Kline, you idiot. You'd better be careful who you stand good for." She lit up again, and sat there nervously taking deep drags from the cigarette, tapping the ashes off constantly with her forefinger.

The Elite Advertising Agency had hired Kutzie Kline, sight unseen, starting her with so much money it worried her. Why they didn't at least interview her, she didn't understand. Only a recent full-length photo of herself was requested, and the very next Monday after she mailed it, Leona Lutz, the owner of Elite, called to ask her to report to work the next Monday. Atlanta is not that far from Charlotte, but it's a chore to even move across town, much less to another city, in another state. She had exactly one week to pack up, move, and start working.

Kutzie packed her car as quickly as she possibly could, tossing everything she could get into it, loose . . . not in boxes, for those would take up too much space and she needed as much as possible in her little Toyota. Elite's promise of $1,000 a week was enough so that she could always straighten everything out after she arrived at her destination. *Why are they going to pay me a salary of $1,000 a week? What am I going to have to do, murder somebody?*

Her main concern was getting to Atlanta, find an apartment, have the electricity turned on, and get a telephone installed in five days. The telephone was of major importance, since her mother was in such bad health. Could she do it? Not if she took her time, and packed things as neatly as she would like to, as was her usual way of doing things. When she kissed her family good-bye that morning, and walked out of the only home she had ever known, she experienced mixed emotions. On one hand, she was sad, even a little depressed. On the other hand and by the time she reached Interstate-85, headed toward Georgia's state capitol, she was as excited as a child with a new toy, almost euphoric as she sped along day-dreaming about her new job.

April is a beautiful time of the year to start a new life, with all the world awakening to brand new flowers, new leaves on the trees, and the birds and the bees busy, and Kutzie was about to start hers. It was the perfect time to arrive in Atlanta and see the native-blooms at the peak of their beauty.

She had hoped one of the decorating companies to whom she had mailed a resume would hire her, but with the good money Elite offered, the advertising business was going to be just fine. Elite was the only company that had acknowledged receiving her resume, anyway.

Kutzie put a cassette tape of Reba McIntyre's "Fancy" in the tape player, and as Reba belted out the words, Kutzie turned up the volume, and sang along with her at the top of her voice. The tape was old and scratchy from being played so many times, but it was still one of her favorites, and Reba was her favorite singer. Many of her friends had told her that she and the lovely singer looked alike, but the resemblance was mostly their hair. Kutzie's was auburn, and very full, and fell past her shoulders. Her eyes were wide, round and emerald green, fringed with long, curly ebony lashes. Her lips were full and pouty, and a dimple played at the corners of her mouth when she talked, or smiled. She was only five-foot-four, compared to Reba's five-foot-seven. One of Kutzie's admirers once told her she had a "Betty Boop" figure, but Kutzie felt she was a tad too skinny, since her waist was a scant twenty-two inches.

Even as she sang her thoughts were on her family, and the impact of leaving them behind had hit her hard only that morning as she prepared to leave Charlotte for good. Her mother was ill, and her father had retired in order to care for her, and Amber, her only sister, was a high school senior working part-time after school at the Public Library. All the family had been concerned over Melissa Kline's declining health during the past two years, as they watched her change dramatically. The simplest thing was a chore for her. She had asked one day where did that television set come from that was in her room? Richard, their father, had explained in his loving patient voice, that it had been there in the living room for years. They found the electric can opener sitting under the sink one day, and assumed it was broken else why would it be there, so Richard bought a new one. The next day the new one was also under the sink, and they were mystified, not realizing at the time that Melissa had hidden them because she didn't know how to use one any longer. As time went on she forgot how to make coffee, when she had made it daily for almost thirty years.

As Kutzie remembered those instances, she felt a pang of guilt because she was moving away at that particular time, when she was probably needed at home more than ever before. The tears began to roll down her cheeks.

She turned off the music, and hit the dash with the palm of her hand. "Damn! Damn," she said aloud, and then slowed the vehicle, turned around, and, headed back east once again, back toward home. She drove along four or five miles with thoughts a-jumble. *What am I doing? I've made up my mind to take that job in Atlanta! I need to start a career! I'm twenty-five years old, and it's time I left home. I'm a grown woman. Besides, I won't be that far from home.* She slowed her car so that she could exit once again, and then crossed the interstate, and headed west again, back toward the Big A town. She couldn't give up such an opportunity, and she didn't want to spend the rest of her life at home living with her parents.

I'll keep in close touch, and if they need me I can be in Charlotte in less than an hour by plane. And, Mom will be getting better soon, anyway.

She turned the radio on again, feeling better about her original decision to accept the job with Elite. As she drove along she was enraptured with the beauty of the mountains. The murky background with its purples, pinks, and black hues was as though mankind had never set foot there before. They were so beautiful, seeming to lack the contamination of the modern world, and its progress.

She turned the volume higher and resumed singing along with Reba, consumed in the intoxicating aroma of the Spring air, as she passed the lush trees, and flowers sprouting along the median. She could hardly wait until she reached Atlanta to see what was awaiting her there. The euphoria she felt was much like waiting to be born!

Of course, she had no idea what her new boss had in store for her . . .

As Kutzie neared the city limits she pulled over to the side of the road to study the map her father had drawn for her to follow when she got into Atlanta. As a salesman before his retirement, Atlanta was a part of his territory, and he knew the town well. She studied it until she was convinced she had it memorized, then slowly eased her little Tercel out onto the busy avenue, driving too slowly, watching carefully for the street where she was to turn. She passed Peachtree Lane, just as a white Corvette whizzed around her, and the driver shot her the finger, as he glared at her. *Hey, Buster, I can drive as fast as you can, but I don't know where I'm going so I'm going slow for a reason, okay?* As the Tercel eased around a corner, she saw it . . . The Elite Advertising Company right there where her father said it would be. The building was impressive in that it was black, and windowless, and seemed to be real marble. She parked inside the garage, and walked inside to the front office. She saw a tanned, blond, manly hunk standing at a file cabinet, wearing a perplexed expression on his handsome chiseled face. She strolled over toward him, and stood quietly watching him, which was most enjoyable. His dark brows were puckered, and he seemed totally in a state of confusion. She stifled the urge to offer to help, but, of course, she couldn't do that. She simply stood there patiently waiting, and enjoying the view. When he wiped a hand across his forehead, he caught a glimpse of her standing there, and smiled. Kutzie was awed. In one glance she took in the hazel eyes, the blond unruly hair, and the beautiful white teeth. The he asked if HE could help HER, and she went blank. *Gads, this guy is the best looking human I've ever seen in my life!* She smiled her prettiest. "I'm Kutzie Kline. I'm supposed to start working here next Monday, but I told Miss Lutz I'd arrive in town today, and would stop by."

His smile broadened, and he leaned over the counter top, offering a big, hairy hand. "Well, hello there, Kutzie Kline.

Leona mentioned your name not even an hour ago. C'mon back to her office, and we'll let her know she can stop worrying now, because you're here."

Kutzie shook hands with him, then he led her down a hall where they entered a large plush office at the end. Because she was interested in interior decorating, Kutzie admired the red chairs, the navy carpet, and the white lamps. A woman who looked to be in her mid-forties was sitting at a massive desk, facing a computer screen, with face screwed up into a frown of disgust as they went in. She mumbled to herself as she typed on the keyboard, then wait, stare at the screen in anticipation, then type something else. Bill cleared his throat, "Excuse me, Leona, Kutzie Kline is here to see you." She didn't budge at first, then squealed in a high-pitched voice. "She is? Where is she? Thank God, she made it!"

Bill took Kutzie's elbow, and gently pulled her toward him, "Here she is . . . the beautiful Miss Kutzie Kline. Leona, meet Kutzie, Kutzie meet Leona," He sounded as if he were enjoying himself.

Leona rose and pushed her chair back forcibly, and hurried around the desk, with both arms outstretched. She grabbed Kutzie's right hand, shaking it with all her might. Not expecting such a rousing welcome on her arrival, Kutzie felt a little silly. Was the woman nuts? What if she were into something she couldn't get out of? She wished Leona would stop shaking her hand so hard. She finally had to pull away, thanking her for her concern, and said that she had enjoyed a good trip without any problems. As the two women talked, Kutzie was aware that Bill stood nearby, smiling to himself as he looked her over, noticing the long tanned legs beneath the short skirt she wore, and her voluptuous torso.

Abruptly, Leona spun around, and walked back to the computer desk, where she sat down, and resumed the typing, and the waiting, and the staring at the screen with the same screwed-up expression on her face. Kutzie hoped the conversation was ended for she had lots to do the remainder of the afternoon. She breathed a sign of relief when she realized that Leona apparently had forgotten about her, and turning to Bill, said, "I need to go so I can find an apartment."

Bill nodded. "I know, and I have a nice place lined up for you to see, Miss Kline, where there's a one-bedroom available." Turning to Leona, he asked, "Do you have any objections if I leave the office for a few minutes, and take Miss Kline around to Chalet Hill Village so she can look at the apartment the manager's holding for her?"

Leona waved an arm, without taking her eyes off the screen. "Go on! In fact, go ahead and leave for the day. It's too close to 4:30 for you to come back to the office. Seems like everything's pretty well wrapped up for the day, anyway." A look of surprise crossed Bill's face. His dark eyebrows arched, and his mouth dropped open. "Why, thank you Boss-lady," he grinned, appreciatively, for it was only a little past noon. Offering Kutzie an arm, he asked, "Shall I lead you back to yon front office, Miss Kline?" He obviously was good-naturedly teasing her. She felt comfortable with the stranger, as though he were her new best friend, and taking the arm he offered, she went along with his teasing. "Yes, please lead me to yon apartment, Sir Knight, for I needeth to unpack my car."

They walked out, without Leona saying 'good-bye', or even looking up from the screen, for she was totally preoccupied, but neither Kutzie nor Bill cared. It was obvious to anyone who might have been there, other than Leona, that they were smitten with each other.

Kutzie gasped with delight when she saw the neighborhood Bill drove to. It was the kind she had dreamed of living in! She had followed Bill less than a mile when he slowed his Lexus before a beautiful, vine-covered apartment complex and pulled in. It sprawled in every direction, nestled among the dogwood trees, not far from aromatic peach orchards. Antebellum homes were in the general neighborhood, and that surprised and impressed her. She noticed that the leaves were full and lush on the trees, and the grass like dark green carpet. Her heart ached as she realized again that this was her first home away from home. Was she happy or sad? A little of both. Anyway, the place was near Elite, and a lovely place to call home.

Bill stopped his car, and she parked alongside him. He opened her door, and they walked toward the 'Information Center', and entered a large open office with a fire burning in the fireplace. The fact that it was warm outdoors was irrelevant, for the embers simply emitted a cozy atmosphere. A middle-aged woman walked out to greet them. When Bill introduced himself first, she acted as if she knew him, ohhing and ahhing about how nice it was to see him. Then, he introduced Kutzie. "She's the lady I told you about that was moving into town, and going to work for us. Her car is loaded to the max, and she needs to move into that available apartment you told me about asap."

The woman smiled, and Kutzie wondered why she didn't have a missing tooth replaced, right in the front. Otherwise, she was quite attractive. "My name is Jan Techwood, Kutzie. I know you're going to love this apartment I'm about to show you. But, first, we have to do a little bit of paperwork. Let me get an application for you to fill out real quick and we'll walk over to see the only apartment I have available right now, and we'll take it from there." Instead of getting the application, she began pointing out the amenities, such as the club room, the outdoor and indoor swimming pools, and the tennis court. Kutzie did not have time to see anything other than the apartment, which Jan must have realized when she saw Kutzie fidget, and quickly said she would take her to see those things later, after she was all moved in, and when they both had more time. Indeed, Kutzie was becoming antsy, and anxious to get her car unloaded. It was dangerous driving it like it was, due to her vision being restricted, because the car was too full. Besides, she needed to find a motel room, and call her parents to let them know she made the trip just fine. Also, she wanted to call the utility companies before they closed for the weekend, or she would be without electricity, and a telephone, and she needed both.

When she completed the information on the application, Jan scanned it quickly, as she chatted.

"Well, Kutzie, normally something like this would take a couple or three days, because we check out our future residents first, but since Mister Davis has stood good for you so to speak, and you're going to be working right over there at Elite, we're going to side-track all of that. Are you ready to see your new home?"

"Yes." Kutzie sighed, and turning to Bill, her lips formed the words, 'thank you'. He smiled, which she took as a 'you're welcome'. Jan locked up the office, and the three of them walked across a flower edged lawn to another building, where she unlocked a large, ornamental door, and stepped aside to allow Kutzie to enter first. Again, Kutzie gasped at the sight. It was small, but lovely. She wrapped her arms around herself, and bubbled with happiness, telling Jan and Bill how thrilled she was with it! They strolled outside so Jan could show her which was her parking space under the carport, assigned to her alone. They hurried back into the office to finalize the lease. "Now, we're going to just take your money," Jan laughed. "We'll need a three-hundred dollar deposit, and we'll pro-rate the rent to the first, so that's going to be a total of five-hundred ten dollars right now. My, this month's already half gone! Seems like this year is flying by."

When Kutzie wrote the check, Jan looked at it, then handed it back, shaking her head. "I'm sorry, but I can't accept an out-of-state check. You'll need either a money order, or a cashier's check."

Kutzie's face fell. She didn't have the time to go buy a money order! Time was of the utmost importance at the moment! Bill took out his checkbook, and quietly wrote a check, and when he handed it to Jan, he turned to Kutzie, and said, "I'll accept your check. I trust you."

Jan handed her the keys to the apartment, along with the receipt for the rent and deposit, and for a brief moment Kutzie stared at them, deluged with feelings of pride and independence, and very appreciative of Bill. "How can I ever thank you?" she asked demurely.

"Just allow me to help you get your car unloaded," he chuckled, rising from his chair.

Together they unloaded it, and everything was in its place in less than an hour, the linens in the closet, dishes in the cupboards, clothes hung neatly in the clothes closets, and her pictures and decorations stashed in the closet for the time being. Exhausted, she turned to Bill, "I can't ask you to sit down and have a seat, since I have none to offer." They laughed, in spite of their fatigue, especially Kutzie. She had done a day's work hours ago.

"As soon as I can get to a payphone," she continued, "I'm going to call my dad, and let him know he can bring my furniture tomorrow. I need to hurry to a phone, so I can call the telephone company and get a phone installed Monday. I want to call home every day and find out how my mom's doing. Also, Jan reminded me to call the electric company as soon as I can, you know."

"You needn't go to a pay phone. Follow me home, and you can use mine. Better still, just leave your car here, and I'll bring you back later."

Kutzie shook her head. "I don't need to come back here, remember? I have no furniture here. That's why I couldn't ask you to sit down, and that's why I have to go find a motel room. But, I'll go find one after I use your phone. I'll gladly take you up on your offer to use it, and, don't worry, I have a phone card to use when I call long distance."

"Hey, don't worry your pretty little head about that either. You can use my phone to call them, and you don't have to use your card. So, follow me, okay? It's really just up the hill from here."

His apartment was nice, although plain, and very masculine. The furniture was clearly pricey, and was mostly in beiges, and browns. Since brown was her least favorite color she was not too impressed. Her first thought was that the living room needed pictures on the walls. Because the carpet was also beige, it didn't do a thing for the apartment in Kutzie's opinion, and she wondered why most men thought they had to use beige and brown? Good old 'earth tones.' She'd love to tell them all that blues and greens is the proper color scheme that most anyone, male or female, should use, besides being relaxing colors. Some day she may offer to help Bill re-do his apartment after they became better acquainted. She smiled when she saw that even his telephone was beige.

First, she called the utility companies, and next, her parents. Her father knew exactly where the apartments were located, and assured her they would see her no later than noon the next day.

When she hung up the phone, and stood up to leave, she

thanked Bill for everything he had done, then picked up her purse, and headed for the door, calling 'good night' over her shoulder.

Bill sputtered. "Hey, wait a cotton-pickin' minute. Neither of us has eaten supper yet, and I hate to eat alone. What say I fix supper for us, while you call the hotels to see what's available? Where were you headed anyway? Do you have some idea where you're going to stay tonight?"

"I noticed a Holiday Inn as I drove into town today. I planned to go there," she answered.

"Wherever you decide is fine, but I think you should call first to ask if they have a room. What if you were to drive over there, and they didn't have a vacancy? Why don't you call and ask, while I fix us something to eat?"

He went into the kitchen, and she called the Holiday Inn. Sure enough, they had a room, and she reserved one, then followed Bill's path to the kitchen. She watched and waited to see what he was going to prepare. He stood at the pantry door staring at the almost empty shelves, and finally took a box of Kraft tangy spaghetti off the shelf. As he peeked into the refrigerator he asked. "Do you like spaghetti? I have a package of ground beef left over." He smelled it. "And, it's still good."

"I love spaghetti," she told him truthfully. "How can I help?"

"Well . . ." he drawled in his southern accent. "If you like onions cooked in your ground beef, I'll cut up a couple, and you put on the water to boil for the spaghetti."

Time passed quickly, while the two of them talked as though they had known each other for years. After they had eaten, they loaded the dishwasher, then sat at the table and continued to talk about every topic under the sun, until Kutzie, as tired as she was after all she had accomplished in one day, stifled a yawn and told Bill she had to go before she fell asleep right there.

"By the way, did I tell you that the phone and the electric will be turned on Monday? Thank heavens for that!"

He nodded, and asked placidly, "Why go to a hotel, anyway, Kutzie? You're welcome to stay here. You can take my bedroom, and I'll sleep on the sofa."

She shook her head. "I can't do that, but I appreciate the offer."

"I'm harmless, I promise." he continued. "Besides, you can stay a little longer, can't you? Later on, you may decide you're too tired to drive anywhere, and you'll go ahead and stay here. I enjoy your company."

"I'm already too tired to drive anywhere else. It's been a long day, and I do have to go."

The offer was tempting, and she was confident he would behave, but it would not be too smart should it ever reach her father's ears! She assured him that she didn't mind going to a hotel, because it was a rare occurrence, thus would be a treat.

She left his place around 8:30, and drove straight to the hotel, and called her parents. Her room was nice and comfortable, and after a warm shower, she went to bed and slept soundly.

It had indeed been a busy day.

The next morning as she drove to her new apartment home she was so absorbed in her thoughts she was not aware of her speed until she noticed the flashing lights behind her. Pulling to the curb she fumed because she had not paid more attention to her driving. She certainly could not afford a citation. She looked through her rear-view mirror, and watched the officer get out of his car, and approach hers. *What a smart-aleck, swaggering as though he's God Himself!*

He touched the brim of his hat, and nodded without even a hint of a smile. "Good morning, Miss. Is there any reason why you're in such a hurry?"

She put on her prettiest smile, and batted her eyes a couple of times as she used to when she practiced before a mirror. In a soft tone, she said, "Not really, Officer. I wasn't aware that I was speeding, although I am quite eager to get home before my parents arrive from Charlotte."

"Let me see your driver's license." His voice was gruff.

She pulled her wallet out of her handbag, and showed him the license. He seemed agitated. "You need to take them out of the wallet, please."

He looked at them then straight at her, and asked, "Do you live in Atlanta or North Carolina?"

Uh oh, I have a North Carolina license, and I just told him that I'm anxious to get home. He thinks he's got me now, for sure. "I'm moving here right now, today. I rented an apartment yesterday, but had to spend last night at The Holiday Inn because I have no furniture here. My parents are bringing it from North Carolina to my apartment this morning."

Please don't give me a ticket!

He excused himself, and walked back to the patrol car while she admired his cute butt in spite of herself, as she watched from her rear-view mirror. When he walked back to her little car, he suddenly smiled as he removed the sunshades, and she looked into sparkling blue eyes that made his entire face suddenly light up. She couldn't believe the transformation from mean to sweet.

"So you're moving to Atlanta?" His voice suddenly seemed to boom when he spoke.

"Yes."

"Do you have a job yet?"

"Yes. I'll be starting to work Monday morning at the Elite

Advertising Company."

"Really? Well, that's not too impressive, if you want my honest opinion."

Hey, did I ask you for an opinion? Besides, you're pretty nosy if you ask me . . .

"What will you be doing there, do you know?" he questioned.

She shrugged her shoulders, "I suppose I'll be learning all there is to learn."

"My ex-wife is in advertising" he went on. "She enjoyed it. At least it seemed like she did since she ran off with the owner of the company she worked for." His tone had turned to a bitter one, and the smile sarcastic.

"I'm sorry," she said, but the thought came to mind, *Why are you telling me your personal business? I don't care to hear it . . .*

"Hey, it isn't a sore spot, anymore. I got over her a long time ago. It's just that the whole sordid incident left a bad taste in my mouth. Do you know anything about your new boss?" His tone was as bitter as his smile, and the sarcasm detected.

"Not much really, but my boss is a female." she quipped. "I stopped by yesterday and met some of the people I'll be working with. I have to admit, though, my boss seems very eccentric."

He chuckled. "Really? I think they all are. What'd she do that gave you that impression?"

"Well, she . . . uh . . . hired me . . . without even meeting me, or interviewing me, which seemed unusual to me . . . it just seemed a little odd. You know? Atlanta is much bigger than my hometown, so why would she hire me, when she doesn't know if I even have good sense? I may be nuts, for all she knows."

"Well, I dunno . . . I guess that is out of the ordinary. Did you mail a resume to the company beforehand?"

"Yes I did."

"Probably you had the best qualifications . . . the most to offer."

"No, I don't think so, because the resume explained that I've had no actual, hands-on experience. Only what I learned in college. Advertising was my minor. I'm simply an apprentice. Besides, she's starting me with a big salary. That's what perplexes me more than anything."

He propped an elbow on the window, and put his chin in the palm of his hand. "If they could have seen you first, they would have hired you on your looks alone."

She smiled, and coyly thanked him, not mentioning that they had requested a recent snap-shot and later, had called to tell her to come to work that very next Monday.

He shuffled around, and then, hesitantly, said, "Tell you what, Kutzie Kline. I won't give you a citation if you'll give me your phone number." He snapped his fingers. "Oh, I forgot. You don't have a telephone yet, since you're just moving to town."

She opened her purse, and took out a small notebook. "The telephone company gave me my number already, but warned me not to have it printed on my personal checks, or anything, until it's actually installed, and working." She handed it to him. He copied the number onto a scrap of paper he pulled from his wallet, and continued to smile at her, and when he handed it back, he winked, and her heart jumped in her chest. *This guy is so darn cute, and sweet.* So far the two men she'd met were very cute. *This is cool!*

"Do you mind if I call you sometime?" he asked. "You did give me the number, so . . ."

She shook her head. "Not at all. In fact, since I don't know anyone here in town, I'm anxious to make friends, and will be looking forward to hearing from you again." And she meant it. He was an all right guy after all, plus he was cute.

He stepped back, and playfully saluted. "See you again, I hope, and you will be hearing from me. Oh, and . . . Miss Kline . . . slow down a little, okay?"

"I will, I promise. And, thank you for not giving me a speeding ticket. I can't afford it!"

Slowly, she pulled out onto the road again, remembering all she had to do. She had to get her apartment arranged as quickly as possible, because once she started working full-time, she wouldn't want to fool with housework when she got home in the evenings. She wondered if she should stop by the grocery store, so she could feed her family when they arrived, but opted not to, lest she not make it home by the time they arrived. She'd take them out to eat, and they would all enjoy that.

Besides she was eager to show-off her new home, her first very own apartment. They would be proud that she had found such a nice place, and in the elite section of Atlanta at that.

As she drove into the complex, her chest swelled with pride. It really was a beautiful place, she realized again, with the trees so tall and majestic, reaching across the boulevard, as well as across the running creek that flowed under the bridge along the jogging trail.

Chapter Two

Kutzie Meets Rusty

She was surprised when she spotted what seemed to be a caretaker of the grounds, working on a Sunday, yet there was a man digging around in the garden with a spade, apparently transplanting flowers. As she passed him he looked up and glared at her with full-blown hatred in his eyes, that caused her to literally shudder. A cold chill shot through her, for she had a feeling he had been watching her. The thought was preposterous however . . . he had never seen her before, and she certainly had never laid eyes on him before! *Who in the world is that? And, why did he look at me like that? He must think I'm someone he knows . . . someone he doesn't like.* Instinctively, she didn't like him either, as she looked back at him through the rear-view mirror. The man was very obese, weighing at least three-hundred, she guessed. His skin was about the darkest she had ever seen, which was conspicuous because his pupils were small and pointed, and his eyeballs very white in contrast. She parked in the carport, and carried her overnight bag into the apartment, unpacked it, and put her things away. No sooner done when the doorbell chimed, and there stood Richard and Amber. Kutzie leaned around to see if her mother was with them. She was not.

"Where's Mom?" she asked, as the smile left her lips.

Her father hugged her, and then Amber, but neither answered her question. Kutzie wondered if they had heard her. "Mom didn't come with you?" she asked a little louder, knowing the answer but asking anyway, disappointment in her voice.

Amber looked at their father, waiting for him to explain, and, he tried. "Kutzie, baby, you mother didn't even know whom we were bringing the furniture to. She told us she was 'afraid' to leave home. We asked Mrs. Becker to come over and stay with her until we get back tonight."

"You mean you're going right back home?" Kutzie suddenly was on the verge of tears. Her voice broke as she spoke. "I expected you to stay over." *Don't they care about me anymore?*

"We have to go back, baby, but we'll be back often to visit you, you can count on that."

"I really hoped you would spend the weekend with me," Kutzie mumbled, "but I know how it is with Mom. Maybe next time she can come with y'all, and stay a week with me."

"It's not that far over here," Amber replied, "I may bring her back to see you next week."

Kutzie dropped to the floor, and put her head in her hands. "Oh, Daddy, it's such an awful disappointment that my own mother wouldn't come over to see my first apartment. I really wanted her to see it, and to be happy for me." She suddenly jumped up, and grabbed him around the neck, and cried, "Not that I wasn't just as anxious for you and Amber to see it, but I wanted to share it with the entire family. I miss Mom so much, and I want her to hurry and get well!"

She started to cry, burying her face into her father's slumped shoulder. He held her silently, and then gently pushed her away from him, and tilted her chin so that she had to look him in the eye. "Listen to me, baby. We all want her to get well, and she's going to, but in the meantime we have to shoulder the load, and realize she doesn't seem to recognize who we are anymore, and can't remember our names most of the time. She's not the way she is because she wants to be, but because she's ill. Very ill." He choked over his words, and began to cry himself. Kutzie was so taken aback, she raised her head and stared at him. His entire body quivered. She patted him on the back awkwardly, and whispered that everything was going to be all right. Amber seemed to be on the verge of crying herself, and left the room hurriedly, and went into another room, calling over her shoulder, "We'd better see where we're going to put all of that stuff, because there's a lot out there! We brought the old living room set, your old bedroom set, and Daddy's old recliner. Plus some little tables, and things I had in my room, that I thought you could use."

Kutzie straightened herself up, and blew her nose into a tissue. "Thanks, Amber. I guess we'd better start bringing it in. Where did you park the U-Haul?"

The three of them walked outside, and Kutzie could hardly believe her eyes when she spotted the fat man again, walking away from the area where her car was parked. She stopped short, and watched, but said nothing to her folks.

Who is that man, and why is he hanging around?

No one else was working on the grounds, and that puzzled her, as she stood and watched to see where he was headed. He walked to a red pickup, and drove out the front gates. She felt better knowing that he was leaving the grounds. For some unexplained reason, she felt very uncomfortable knowing that he had been there.

"Kootie! Whatcha doing?" Amber called from inside the van, and laughing, Kutzie ran on out to the U-Haul to help unload it, forgetting about the stranger for the time being. She tweaked Amber on the nose, saying, "Hey, why don't you start calling me 'Kutzie' now, okay?"

An hour later, the van was unloaded, and Kutzie was arranging the apartment the way she had planned it out in her head earlier. When they were all done, and the van was totally emptied, they sat down, tired and wiping their brows. Kutzie ran to the kitchen, and brought back big frosted glasses of iced tea, informing them she wanted to take them out to lunch since she had not taken the time to stop by the grocery store as she drove home from the hotel that morning. She told them how she had almost gotten a citation for doing forty-five in a thirty-five mile zone. Richard cautioned her about driving too fast in Atlanta, because the policemen there are always on their toes, he said, and would catch anyone that was breaking the law in a New York minute. Kutzie told him that the patrolman was nice enough not to give her a ticket, but she didn't mean to speed of course. She simply didn't have her mind on how fast she was going at that particular time.

They each took their turns to shower, changed into fresh clothing, and Kutzie drove to a nice restaurant, following her father's directions, and they enjoyed a wonderful early dinner together.

Afterwards, Richard and Amber left to return to Charlotte. Kutzie missed them very much, but she was not sorry she had accepted the job with Elite and had moved away. She was comfortable with her original decision to move out, and get her own place. That night as she watched television all alone, she loved the total, real independence she felt. Moving to a place of her own had been a long-time dream of hers, and she felt older and more mature.

Sunday was a lovely day with lots of sunshine, although cool. The beautiful azaleas, and, the dogwoods were a sight to behold. Spring filled the air, as Kutzie drove to the grocery store, buying mostly snacks. She didn't plan to cook big meals just for herself. She put the groceries away, and then finished unpacking the boxes her father had brought with him. She spent the rest of the day decorating her apartment exactly right, exhilarated as she did everything.

Later, she took a shower, shampooed her hair, blow-dried it, and went to bed with a book on 'decorating', which she did not get a chance to read because she fell asleep almost immediately.

Monday Morning as Kutzie dressed for work, she was

undecided on what to wear her first day. She finally decided on a navy blue denim suit, with a red and white striped blouse, navy stockings with navy shoes. She swirled her hair up on top of her head, which made her look older than her twenty-five years. Looking more like a fashion model than a working girl, she walked briskly into the Elite building in her two-and-a-half-inch heels, and all heads turned as she passed.

Leona looked up as Kutzie entered the room, and as she looked her over, her red lips spread into a wide smile. "You dressed the part perfectly, Dear. That skirt is just short enough to be just right, yet it's very business-like. I like that. Now, here's what I want you to do, and it's what I hired you to do. We have a department store here in town by the name of Hubbard's. We've been trying for years to get the store's advertising business, but the manager of the store, who happens to also be the owner, won't even talk to any of us, because he isn't interested in changing to a new ad agency. That's where you come in. I've made up my mind we are going to get their account, and you're the one to do that for us. The man is a bachelor, and your job is to do what you have to do, all that you need to do, if you know what I mean. But, get Hubbard's account, or else! Now, there's a mapsco on your desk highlighted on how to get to the store. Oh, let me show you your office, and then you get ready to go on to Hubbard's." She clicked her heels, as she walked down the carpeted hall, and Kutzie wondered how she did that. Suddenly, it dawned on Kutzie what Leona had said about getting that account, or else. "What do you mean to do what I have to do, or else? What do you think I am anyway? This job doesn't mean so much that I'll stoop to doing certain things for it. I don't need it that much!" Kutzie was pissed, and made no bones about it.

"I'm sorry for what I said. I guess I'm over-anxious. The store opens at ten sharp, you be there at nine-fifty-nine, waiting." Leona replied, her eyes squinted. Kutzie wondered if she were angry or had eye problems. Kutzie followed Leona into a large room. "Here's your office." Kutzie was impressed, because of the exquisite furniture in it. She sat down in the tall chair, and spun around without realizing how childish it seemed to Leona who was not the least amused. She slapped the mapsco into Kutzie's palms, and told her not to forget to take it with her and to go ahead and go on over.

Kutzie knew where the store was. She had passed it on her way into town Friday, and remembered she was entranced at its beauty and uniqueness. It was so large, it took up about two blocks at least. While driving over, she wondered about the owner of Hubbard's. He had to be an old coot set in his ways, and stubborn as a mule. If she didn't get the account, she figured that would be the end of her advertising career from the way

Leona talked. Well, if she lost that job she could get another one easy enough, although not one that would start her with a salary of $1,000 a week, that much she was sure of. Would she resort to 'whatever it takes' to keep her job?

She looked at the store directory, and rode the escalator up to the third floor. The secretary buzzed Mister Hunt on the intercom, who said he was sorry but he was too busy to see anyone without an appointment. Kutzie thought to herself: *Who does he think he is anyway? Why should a customer have to make an appointment to see the store manager?* She'd show him, the old smartie. She walked away, thought about what she would do, then went back and told his secretary that she had a complaint, and wished to speak to the manager.

"Maybe I can help you?" the secretary suggested.

"Are you the manager?" Kutzie asked in a voice which indicated that she meant business.

"No. I'll buzz him again. I've forgotten what you said your name was?"

Kutzie told her again what her name was, and the woman called Rusty Hunt on his intercom.

"Miss Kutzie Kline has a complaint, and insists on speaking with you."

His voice was deep, and resonant on the intercom, as he simply said, "Okay, send her in."

When Kutzie sauntered into his office, one hip following the other, she was disappointed he wasn't even looking her way as she entered. He was sitting in a large office chair at his huge desk with his head down so far she couldn't see what he looked like, other than he had dark hair, instead of the gray she expected. He was flipping through papers that were on his lap, and never looked up when he mumbled, "Have a seat."

How rude! I can tell right off the bat that you're an old grouch, and I don't like you already.

When he did finally look up, she did a double-take. He wasn't old at all. He did not look at all as she expected. In fact, he looked almost boyish when he smiled, flashing pearly-whites, embellished with a small, dark mustache above the lip. He reminded her of some movie star, but . . . who?

"Please have a seat, Miss Kline. What can I do for you? I'll do all I can to remedy the problem, whatever it is."

She crossed her legs as she sat down, and put on her friendliest smile. "I'm from the Elite adver . . ."

That was as far as she got, when the smile left his face. "You deceived me into thinking I was to rectify a complaint when you're from that blasted advertising agency that keeps bugging me to advertise with them?" He sounded really angry. "What does it take to convince them that I'm not interested? Get that? NOT! Period!"

Not expecting such an outburst, she began to cry. "I'm sorry. I didn't realize . . .", and taking a tissue from her purse she dabbed her eyes, and blew her nose.

He was bewildered. His face fell, and he jumped to his feet, and hurried around the desk to her. But then he stopped, and just stood there not knowing what to do or say. He raised his eyebrows, and shoved both hands into his pockets. "Good grief, why are you crying?"

She looked up at him, her eyes wide and innocent, bottom lip puckered, and between sobs, she whispered, "Because I'm going to be fired if you don't at least allow us to prove that we can improve your business. I only started working there this morning. I moved here from Charlotte just this past weekend, and I need this job . . ."

"Hey, wait a second here." He walked back around to his chair, and sat down. "Back up a little. What in the world do you mean, you'll lose your job if you don't get my ad account? This store can't be so important that you'd lose your job unless you get our advertising business?" Rusty Hunt's eyes were narrowed, as he spoke, and he seemed angry all over again.

"But, it's true!" She realized she sounded childish. "I don't know why, but that's what I was told."

He glared at her, as though he was shocked, then stood again, and began pacing the floor. After a couple of go-rounds he sat down again, rubbing his chin, and his voice suddenly became very kind. "I don't know what to tell you, Miss Kline. You see, the agency I use at present belongs to a relative. My father's brother. That's the reason I can't change."

"Oh, no! I knew there had to be a good reason," she fibbed. She crossed her shapely long legs again, carefully placing one in front of the other properly, so as not to reveal too much thigh. Out of the corner of one eye, she saw that he was watching her every move. She dabbed at her eyes once in a while with the tissue, and quietly, and daintily blew her nose.

Without warning, he suddenly hit his desk with a fist, startling her. His teeth were clamped together, and his dimples deepened on either side of his mouth. She sat upright in the chair, and with eyes stretched she watched him, electrified for he was exciting. His thick dark hair was mussed somewhat, because he had run his fingers through it at least a half-dozen times while pacing. He stopped suddenly, and looked straight into her green eyes, and with a half-smile, asked, "What would you do if you were in my shoes?"

The question surprised her, but she decided to take advantage of the situation, and play it up for all it was worth, which in this instance happened to be her job.

Tossing her head, she wished for a fleeting second that she had worn her hair down, thinking how long hair usually impressed the men in her life, and for sure, she wanted to impress him.

"I would stay with the relative. Family ties are too important."

His smile widened, and suddenly, she remembered who he looked exactly like. The movie star who starred in a movie she once saw on television a few years back; Clark Gable! The movie was, "Gone With the Wind".

Her answer obviously surprised him, for he asked with that same wide smile, "Really?"

"Absolutely. I love my family and wouldn't want anyone creating problems between us."

"Well, I can hardly believe my ears. You sound as if you mean that."

Leaning back in his chair, he looked at her for a minute without saying anything, and she gazed back at him, eyes level, without quandary. His entire attitude seemed to change, she noticed. He propped his chin into the heel of his hand, and looking serious, replied, "Well, let me think about this. Can I call you later on?" Inwardly she smiled with satisfaction. Was this the mean old man she had been warned about? She put on her sweetest smile. "Of course you may."

She offered her right hand as she stood up, and he shook it, smiling. When she slipped her hand from his, she reached into her purse, and handed him a business card. "I don't have my own cards just yet, of course, but just ask for me, and I'll be happy to bring over some lay-outs."

"I'll certainly consider it." he promised, and she felt his eyes on her backside as she walked away and walked to the escalator.

Whether to be disappointed or elated, she was not sure. But there was hope, and she was definitely going to do the job she was hired to do as best she could. Working with Rusty Hunt was going to be just about perfect. On her way back to the office she began planning on what to do next to change the man's stubborn mind, should he not call after a few days elapsed. She'd think of something for sure.

She breezed into Leona's office with confidence literally exuding from every step she took.

Leona, sensing the mood, smiled broadly, revealing lipstick-stained teeth. "What? What? Did you get the account? Tell me what he said to you."

Kutzie perched on the edge of the desk, and spread her open hand, eyeing her nails.

"Well, of course there was nothing definite decided on, I'm sorry to say, but at least, I talked with him."

"Tell me everything that was said." Leona gushed breathlessly. At that moment, an employee whom Kutzie had not met, walked into Leona's office with a stack of papers in her hands. "Pardon me, Leona, but I needs your advice . . ." she began. Leona whirled around, and snapped at the young woman, "Can't you see that Kutzie and I are engaged in an important conversation, Bess? Take those into Treva, and ask her to help you with whatever the hell you've got there!"

The woman glared at Kutzie with narrowed eyes, turned on her heel, and stormed out.

What was that all about? Kutzie wondered. Why was the dirty look directed at her? Oh, well . . . She continued telling Leona what she and Rusty Hunt had discussed. She didn't mention that she had cried, nor that she told him she would lose her job without the account. She explained only that Mr. Hunt's uncle owned the agency that Hubbard's presently employed. Leona replied, with feeling, "Oh, damn! So that's why he's been so stubborn." Kutzie then said that Mr. Hunt had promised to consider her request, and contact her later.

At that moment, Kutzie heard a conversation outside Leona's office, and thinking it was Bill, excused herself, saying she should go into her own office, and get started on some ads that Mister Hunt might be interested in if he should call. She really wanted to say 'hello' to Bill, but when she walked out into the hall, she saw that it was not Bill at all, but an older man attempting to explain something to the woman who had interrupted Leona a few moments earlier. He was plainly agitated with her, as he said angrily, "That's not the kind of ad the customer requested, Bess, I told you that." And then, Bess' high-pitched voice, "So what do you suggest then? I'm not a mind reader, you know. If Leona wasn't so wrapped up with that prissy little bitch she just hired, *she* could show me."

Kutzie felt her face grow hot with fury, and leaning against the wall, she stood there with one hand on a hip, until Bess turned around to see her standing there. Kutzie's eyes flashed. "I'm glad you detected that I'm a bitch." she said through tight lips. "Just remember that!" And, she turned, and prominently displayed her prissy walk, as she returned to her office. Bess, obviously embarrassed, stared at Kutzie without saying a word. Slightly agitated that the woman had called her a bitch causing her to react in a manner she had not realized she was capable of, Kutzie determined to put the incident out of her mind. Undoubtedly, Bess was the type to blame others for her mistakes, but, at least she had let her know she would not tolerate being walked on, just because she was the new kid on the block.

She seated herself at her new desk, and rubbed her palms over it, feeling privileged to have the use of such a fine piece of furniture, just as Bill walked into the room, humming a little tune. She whirled around to see who came in, and, at first glance thought, *Hello, you good-looking thing you!* He looked even better that day than on Friday if that were possible. She drank in his handsome features, as he smiled, and sat down beside her desk. She looked him over, noticing the expensive clothes he wore; the well-tailored gray slacks, with a gray and white striped shirt, complimented with a red tie. His shoes were shiny black. The blond hair was neatly combed, and tame. She had a thought that running her fingers through it would be nice. She pondered on which of the two was the better-looking . . . Rusty or Bill? Rusty might be better-looking. It was hard to compare which of the two was more so. Probably Bill was. He was a dream-come-true deluxe.

"Are you getting your phone turned on today for sure?" he queried.

She nodded. "As far as I know. I was told it would be turned on sometime today, you remember, and that was the last thing they said to me."

"I don't want to forget to get the number from you, okay?" Stifling a yawn, he apologized, saying, "I'm beat! I had nightmares about you all night long. Some man was chasing you, and I was chasing him, and I've been tired all day from all that running."

Kutzie laughed.

"How did Saturday and Sunday go?" he wanted to know. "I thought about you all weekend, assuming your folks brought your furniture and that y'all had a nice visit while they were here?"

She frowned. "My mom wasn't able to make the trip, and a friend stayed with her. Just my dad and sister came and went back home Saturday evening. But, I had an opportunity to at least get settled, except for a couple of boxes that I'll unpack later. And I almost got a speeding ticket while driving back to my apartment Saturday morning. But the officer was very nice."

Nibbling on the tip of a pen, she added, "At least, my apartment has furniture in it, so it's homey. You'll have to come see it. Oh, I forgot to give you the number the phone company gave me Friday evening. They warned me not to have it printed on anything, until it's installed. But, since they didn't call today, I'm assuming it's going to work just fine. Here it is."

He took it. "Thanks. As for my coming over, you just say when and I'll be there." He folded the paper, put it in his shirt pocket, and walked toward the door. "I'll call you later, okay?"

* * *

The first working day was not at all what Kutzie had expected it to be. She thought back on the day's events while driving home: the conversation she and Rusty Hunt had regarding Elite; the person Bess, who had called her a bitch, about Leona's unusual and emotional behavior. *Really a strange individual!* She thought back to what the police officer had said, and, as always, she thought of her mother, and how she wished she could understand what was going on with her mom's strange illness.

As soon as she walked into her apartment, she picked up the telephone hoping to hear a dial tone. She did. She called Charlotte, and her dad seemed surprised to hear her voice, but he should KNOW that she would call again, as soon as she had telephone service, she thought.

"Hello, Baby." he seemed genuinely glad to hear her voice.

"Dad, my telephone's connected! I gave you and Amber the number on Saturday, didn't I?"

He affirmed that she had.

"I had to call and ask about Mom. Is she feeling any better?"

"Well, would you like to speak to her? She's right here. Tell her about your new job."

"Oh, I will. Okay, put her on."

"Yeah." It was her mother's voice.

"Mom, it's Kutzie! I wanted to tell you about my new job here in Atlanta."

"Yeah."

"Mom, I want you to come visit me sometimes soon, will you?"

"Yeah."

"Are you feeling okay? Miss me?"

"Yeah."

Why, Mom, why? Oh, Mom, you don't even understand what I'm saying! This is such a disappointment, knowing you don't even recognize my voice.

"Mom, may I speak to Dad again?"

"Yeah."

"Mom, please put Richard on the phone."

"Yeah."

The experience was so exasperating, she started to cry, and then she heard her father's voice.

"Kutzie? Sweetheart, I don't think your mother can carry on a telephone conversation anymore. I guess I just didn't realize . . ." She detected the break in his voice and could almost see a tear in his eye.

"I know, Dad." She got a grip on her emotions. "Well, just take good care of her and when the doctor's determine what the illness is, maybe then they can start curing it. I just want her to get well so much."

After talking awhile they hung up, and Kutzie sat in the big recliner that once was her dad's, and thought back on the time when they first took Melissa to a doctor. He diagnosed her problem as old age syndrome . . . premature senility. Richard Kline did not accept that diagnosis, for his wife wasn't old enough to be senile. She was only 50.

The day before Kutzie left Charlotte for Atlanta, he took Melissa to a geriatric specialist, who performed an MRI test. The results of the tests would be known within the next couple of days, and Richard had promised his daughter he would let her know the results as soon as they heard.

Kutzie forced herself to go into the kitchen, and make herself a sandwich even though she was not hungry at all. It was already six-thirty, but food did not seem appealing. She poured herself a glass of milk, and went back into the living room and turned on a game show called, "Wheel of Fortune", hoping she would feel better watching happy contestants win prizes. She did little else that evening, finally took a hot bath, hit the sack, but could not sleep. She tossed and turned fitfully all night long.

When Kutzie arrived at work the next morning, she found Leona waiting, mouth spread wide showing lipstick stains on her teeth as usual. "Kutzie, Rusty Hunt called a few minutes ago. He wants you to meet him at his office at 10:00 this morning. Now, don't you be late for that appointment! I have a feeling it's going to be good news for Elite!"

Kutzie smiled with delight. "Really? That's wonderful. I wonder what he's going to tell us? I asked for a chance to prove we can increase the store's business, and promised him that we positively could, you know? We've got to deliver!"

"I don't give a little damn what you had to tell him, as long as he'll use us for their ad biz, and don't you worry your red head about our deliverance. That's my job."

* * *

Rusty Hunt was sitting in the large leather chair at his mahogany desk when Kutzie entered his office. He motioned for her to have a seat, and then with hands folded before him he simply looked at her and grinned. "I've been giving it a lot of thought, and I don't want you to lose your job and force you to leave Atlanta."

She flashed the emerald green eyes, and her lips parted. "You mean . . . ?"

Well, when I arrived home yesterday I couldn't believe it, but there was a letter from my Uncle Nick. He's planning to retire, and has his agency up for sale. Is that fate or what, Miss Kline? I think that Somebody upstairs likes you, and must want me to hire Elite to do an ad or two for the store."

She laughed giddily, "I can hardly believe it myself. What perfect timing. You don't know how much I appreciate it. Thank you very much, Mister Hunt. I don't want to get fired that's for sure."

She was glad she had worn her hair down that morning, for

it was bouncy, soft, and full, and she caught him eyeing it as he said, "Well, let's go get a cup of coffee, and discuss what the first ad will consist of, shall we?" He shoved a batch of papers to the back of his desk and stood up."

"Have you eaten anything?"

She shook her head, "Not even a bowl of cereal."

"We have a coffee shop downstairs. We can grab a bite of breakfast there, and go somewhere else later for lunch. Did you happen to bring any ad samples with you? We can discuss our business in a corner of the coffee shop."

"As a matter of fact, I did some sketches yesterday afternoon, and I have them inside my briefcase right now." She answered, pondering on what he had just said about the coffee shop now and lunch later. Was he going to spend most of the day talking business, when he was not even willing to discuss it at all the day before?

Chapter Three

Rusty Hunt Steals Kutzie's Heart

She beamed with pride, as she walked beside him out of his office, and to the elevator. She pulled the straps of her purse onto her shoulder as she said, "Leona told me I could spend as much time as necessary with you today. Wasn't that sweet of her?"

He laughed, as he helped her with the straps. "And, if you don't spend time with him, Kutzie Kline, you're fired. Right?"

"Something like that," she admitted.

He had his hand to her back as they rode down on the elevator, and she tingled at his gentle, magic touch. 'Magic' because of the rare fire she felt inside her. She had been labeled as cold and insensitive and a touch-me-not when she went out with her 'childhood boyfriends' back home in Charlotte.

She was happy that their relationship had gotten off on the right foot, because Rusty knew now how Leona was, and they could joke about things like her firing Kutzie if she didn't bring Rusty Hunt's head in on a platter. He mentioned that while they were eating in the coffee shop, and the two of them enjoyed a good laugh over it.

Even though he had mentioned they could sit in a corner to talk business and discuss the sketches she had drawn, the subject somehow never came up. Instead, he asked about her life in Charlotte before Elite, and she in turn, asked about his life before Hubbard's. She told him about attending NCSU, whom her best friends were, about the volunteer work she had done at a local hospital and that she had also worked part-time for a small advertising business. She laughingly mentioned the intern she once dated who proposed marriage but fell for one of her friends when she introduced him to her friend, Crystal, who was hospitalized where he was on duty.

He told her how his parents traveled all over the world since his father's retirement, after he had turned Hubbard's over to him. About his brother Chris' recent engagement to a girl named Andrea whom he met when he moved to Phoenix to work for their Uncle Nick in the Advertising Agency. Chris had no interest in Hubbard's at all, but was interested in advertising for awhile, until he opened his own business in Phoenix, a line of clothing, and had become very successful. Because he played golf, he enjoyed the Phoenix weather year-round, and he planned to remain there. Reared in Dallas, Texas, graduates from SMU, neither had ever thought of leaving Texas. Their father Charles, was a successful attorney in Highland Park, and his mother, Lana, was a Socialite. When Hubbard Hunt died, Nick and Charles were his only heirs, but neither had any interest in the department store. Eventually Charles gave up his career as an attorney, and managed Hubbard's for awhile after he and Lana moved to Atlanta, until Rusty graduated from Southern Methodist University. Uncle Nick had sold his inherited half of the store to Charles, and it was at that time that they agreed to do business with each other, which he continued to do.

After Rusty's graduation, his father sold him the business free and clear, allowing him to make payments out of the store's profits. He proudly told her he had also bought Grandfather Hunt's home in Atlanta the same way he bought the store; out of the store's profits. Even though he had thought at one time that he would remain in Dallas for the rest of his life, Atlanta was all right, because much of it reminded him of Dallas, although it was smaller than Big D. They owned their home in Highland Park still, and occasionally his parents would return there for a few days before jetting off to another country.

"There now. I think I've told you more about myself than I've ever told anyone before." Rusty grinned. "And, do you realize we've been in this coffee shop for two hours? I've drunk more cups of coffee since we came in here than I've drunk in a month."

"Me, too." Kutzie admitted.

"Where can we go from here? We need to talk." His one-sided smile was very cute, she mused.

Talk? They had talked two hours. She told him so.

"Well, we need to discuss the matter of this advertising stuff, don't we?" he asked. She had to laugh. They left the coffee shop, and went to the parking garage, where Rusty's car had been brought up; a gorgeous white Rolls-Royce. When she sat down, she sank into the luxurious leather seat, sighing. He eased the car out onto the avenue, and into the bright sunlight, and when Kutzie took a pair of sunshades from her purse and put them on, he watched as she did so, then said, "I know that's the right thing to do, wear shades when out in the sun, but now your beautiful eyes are covered and I'm disappointed. I think your eyes are fascinating."

"Why, thank you, Mister Hunt." She dimpled, but she didn't remove the shades.

She could hardly keep her eyes off his profile, as they drove along Peachtree Drive. He was quite good-looking, possessing the strong features she admired in a man. His hands were big, and masculine, as he confidently wielded the automobile through the noon traffic that was beginning to become congested. She saw that his bottom teeth showed more than his top ones did when he talked, and his dimples deepened and that captivated her. He asked if she would like to drive to Babyland General Hospital to see where the Cabbage Patch babies were created, and she agreed that it would be fun. It was a beautiful drive over to Cleveland, Georgia, especially in the month of April. When they arrived at the Cabbage Patch Hospital, again he held a hand to her back as they made their way inside. The hospital was interesting to walk through, and Kutzie was at ease with Rusty, as he held her hand while they walked through.

Charlotte was too near Cleveland, GA for her to have never been to Babyland General Hospital before, she mentioned to Rusty, and added with finesse, how nice that he was the one who took her to see it the first time. She detected his pride when she paid him the compliment.

They were laughing as though they had known each other forever, as they walked to the car, and Rusty asked, "Do you feel any differently knowing they named one of their newborn baby's 'Kutzie', and now you've become a 'mother'?"

"I do have a namesake, don't I? I didn't know that's how the Cabbage Patch babies are named. And gosh, Mister Hunt, that was fun!" No sooner had she used the childish expression . . . 'gosh' . . . when she wished she hadn't. She wanted to stop using those 'little-girl' words she used to, and to become more sophisticated now that she was a grown woman out on her own.

"Kutzie, please. 'Mister' sounds so formal. Just call me Rusty, and let me call you Kutzie? I think we're too young to be Mister and Miss when we talk to each other."

"How old are you?" She inquired, always curious. "I'm twenty-five, myself."

"I'm thirty, turning thirty-one on January twelfth. See? We're too young to be a Mister and Miss . . . We're young squirts."

He reached for her hand again as they walked on to the car, as though it were the most natural thing in the world to do. As he drove back to Atlanta, he detoured so that he could show her some of the famous landmarks her father had talked about through the years and she had hoped one day to see.

Around 1:30 they stopped at The Westin Peachtree Plaza,

because Rusty wanted to show her the tallest hotel in America. Kutzie was awed by the unique lobby, and all the sights there to see.

The walk through the doll hospital had whetted their appetites, and they were famished. Rusty suggested they have lunch in the revolving rooftop restaurant. While eating, they once again spoke of their families, all the while getting to know each other better. When she told him about her mother's illness, she could not help her eyes brimming with tears. A look of concern crossed his handsome face. "Kutzie, that sounds like Alzheimer's. One of my former employees is a victim of it. It's a terrible, debilitating disease, and if that's what you mom has your entire family is going to need counseling. Mrs. Graves had to retire last year when she was only fifty-three, because she could no longer remember how to do certain things. She started out by forgetting how to run the register, and then she became confused about how to do other duties she had always performed on a daily basis for years. Her husband mentioned that he had noticed for two or three years little things she did or said, that were not normal. She's in a nursing home today."

Kutzie had already suspected her mother may have Alzheimer's, for she remembered reading about its symptoms which fit her mother perfectly. She had also read about the movie star, Rita Hayworth, having it several years ago. Now, it was very real to her, especially since Rusty had described it to a T, and she knew she was going to have to face it if that's what her mother had, no matter how she may not want to.

"What causes it?" She had to choke the words out. "Does anyone know?"

"I don't think so." Rusty said softly, "But much research is being done on it every day."

She dropped her eyes, and chewed her bottom lip. "The way you described Mrs. Graves is the way Mom is. She seems not to know any of the family anymore. She can't even carry on a conversation. Oh, Rusty, this is so hard to accept!" She dropped her forehead onto the palm of one hand, and when Rusty said simply, "I'm sorry," he lay a hand over her other one.

* * *

As Kutzie drove back to Elite that afternoon, she smiled to herself that nothing had been accomplished as far as business was concerned, but she had learned a lot about Rusty Hunt that was very interesting, and made her only want to know him better. In fact, when he mentioned they should get together again the next day and discuss ads for sure, the hair stood up on her neck for she ached to see him again! The feeling that she had must mean she was falling in love with him! Yet, the thought was preposterous. How could she love him already?

He was so sweet! *I hope this means he likes me . . . I need a man like that.*

She didn't want Leona to know that she had spent the day gallivanting about in Cleveland, GA touring the doll hospital, when she did not get back to the office until almost 4:30 in the afternoon, for she surely would not appreciate that it was a part of her job of ad selling.

As she stepped out of her car in Elite's garage, she glimpsed the fat man she had seen working in the garden at her apartment complex on Sunday! *What's he doing HERE at Elite? WHO is the man anyway?* He saw her, started running, and ducked behind an automobile. She spotted quick movements of him as he ran, stooped, through the parked cars. She put both hands on her hips and watched him dart between the cars, as he ran toward the exit. She didn't understand why he was suddenly turning up everywhere she happened to be. A coincidence? Not likely, for why had he showed up at her home, and now, her work place? She would feel better if Bill knew what was going on, and she was going to tell him immediately. She went inside the building hurriedly, as though something were pushing her, and went directly into her office.

She had not realized that she ran all the way in from the garage, until breathing hard and completely out of breath, she had to sit a moment to rest. She was frightened as well, and that was one reason for her hard breathing. Leona walked in without the big smile she usually greeted her with, asking soberly, "Well, Kutzie, how did it go today? What did you get accomplished?"

Kutzie presumed she was angry because she had been out of the office all day, and hadn't called, but the thought had not occurred to her at all to call.

She answered in a calm voice, "I think we're going to settle it all tomorrow. He wants to see more lay-outs before deciding anything definite. He's not easy to convince, Leona."

Then came the lipstick smile. "But, you think he will, don't you? Don't you think he's about ready to hire our agency?"

Kutzie brushed a lock of the dark auburn hair back from one eye, and answered complacently. "He didn't say anything definite. I just hope I can convince him within the next few days. Sometimes I think he's weakening, but then I think I may have to do a little arm-twisting. Or whatever I need to do." *There! That should make her feel better, making her think I'll stoop to doing most anything to get the business for the company.*

Leona practically floated out of the office, high on gratification. Kutzie watched her, shaking her head in disbelief. A tap on the door caused her to look up, and there stood Bill, with that perfect smile on his good-looking face. "May I come in?" he asked, looking like a young clone of Robert Redford.

She smiled, "Of course you may. Have a seat. We have about five minutes before we leave for the day."

"I wondered if you were going to make it back before quitting time. I've been expecting you to walk through that door for the last hour!"

"Do you mean to say you missed me?" she teased.

"Strange, isn't it? I can't believe it myself." His smile was a half-hearted one, as he brushed a hand through his blond hair. "Just think," he continued, "a week ago I never even knew you, other than you were going to come to work for Elite. Now, this place isn't the same without you. Crazy, isn't it? But, yes, I missed you. But, hey, you were gone all day!"

She threw back her head and laughed. "Bill, that's sweet of you to say that. You're full of it, but I enjoy hearing things like that."

As they left Elite they agreed they should have dinner somewhere together, and Bill followed her home. She parked her car under the carport and Bill stopped beside her, opened her door, and helped her into his Lexus. He leaned over as she buckled the seat belt, and whispered into her ear. "Did I mention that you look lovely today?"

"Bill, you're just so complimentary, I don't know what to say. But, I love it."

"I assure you I don't say things like that unless I mean them. As you get to know me, you'll see that I don't flatter anyone. I say what I think. And, I think you're gorgeous."

As they sped away, he said. "There now, isn't it easier to talk to each other when we're in the same car? You probably wouldn't have heard a word I said if you were following me in your car."

She cracked up when she caught on to the joke. She loved his sense of humor.

He drove to the Cracker Barrel Restaurant, and they shopped in the store area while waiting on a table. When they sat down, they laughed when they were stumped while playing with the puzzle the restaurant provided on each table for their customers.

Later, at home, Kutzie relived the enjoyable time she had spent with him at the restaurant although they had done nothing in particular, except laugh at nothing. It was good that they felt so comfortable with each other, as if they had known each other for years. The phone rang, interrupting her thoughts. She was surprised to hear Bill's voice. "Hey, Gorgeous, I haven't talked to you in so long, I thought I would call and see how you're doing?"

"Oh, Bill, you silly you." He was such a clown.

"I wanted to ask you out next Saturday night. I'd like to take you dancing. I meant to ask before I took you home but I was so enamored being in your presence, I completely forgot about it until I walked inside my door."

She giggled. "Well, I plan to go shopping Saturday evening, Bill. Margo's is having a shoe sale only between the hours of 6:00 p.m., and 8:00 p.m., and I want to take advantage of that. But, I really would love to go. Could I meet you somewhere after 8:00, 8:30?"

"Well, as I said earlier, I'd rather have a conversation with my date while we're in the same car, but your way is better than no way at all. I suppose we can meet at Studebaker's if you enjoy 50's and 60's music? I'll be there waiting. I'd really rather pick you up at your apartment around 8:30 or 9:00 though . . ." he begged.

"No, it isn't necessary to do that when I'll be out shopping anyway," she interrupted. "Draw a map showing how to get to Studebaker's and give it to me tomorrow, and I'll meet you after I do my shopping. Is the place fairly easy to find?"

"Yeah, but I'll draw a map you can't misunderstand in any way form or fashion, I promise. We can also have dinner there. It's over on Peachtree. It's real easy to find."

He told her how much he enjoyed having supper with her at the restaurant and again how he disliked eating alone, and that he wouldn't mind at all making a habit of it. They hung up when her other line rang. It was the policeman who had stopped her for speeding last Sunday. "Well, the phone number does work, doesn't it?" She heard a man's laugh. "This is Ricky Larson. How are you? Haven't gotten any speeding tickets lately, have you?"

"So that's your name. You didn't tell me who you were last Saturday, you know. I didn't know if I would know it was you when you called." *How childish to say such a thing!* she thought to herself. She was happy to hear from him again, and said so. He asked how things were going at her new job and she told him of the challenge she had been given, and how it looked very hopeful.

"Well Kutzie, I called to ask if you'd like to go out Saturday night? I've been waiting quite impatiently for today to arrive so I could call you and ask."

"I'd love to, Ricky, but, I have a date Saturday night."

"You do? That's not really a surprise even though you're new to Atlanta. I hoped to be your first Atlanta date." He laughed again. "Someone you work with?"

"Yes. A sweetheart of a guy. He helped me find this apartment, and even talked the manager into letting me move in without checking me out first, since my car was loaded to the gills. You should have seen it! You would've cited me for obstructed vision. He's been super nice in a lot of different ways . . . a lot of help to me."

"Oh, yeah? Well, that was darn nice of him. Is he an older

man?"

What difference does that make? "No. About twenty-six, thirty at most. Why?"

"I dunno. I guess that sounds like something an older person would do. Oh, well, how about Monday night? We could go to a movie. I wouldn't keep you out late on a work night. I have to work Sunday night myself, so I can't ask you to go out then, but Monday is the soonest for me." She said Monday night was just fine. They talked awhile before they hung up, and Kutzie felt a sense of belonging in this new home-town of hers, because she had made new friends already.

Wednesday morning was dark and dismal-looking when she awoke and thought it was not quite daylight. She remembered hearing something on the news the night before about a chance of thunderstorms. She turned on the radio by her bedside and heard immediately that tornadoes were predicted. She wasn't afraid of stormy weather, but she preferred not to be out in it. She dressed, and left for work a little earlier than usual, and ran into heavy rain just before she reached Elite.

She hurried inside, thankful for the protection of the garage. Rusty Hunt called at 8:30 sharp. "I had to see if you made it to the office all right. Any problems?" she caught the relief in his voice when she answered the phone. "Oh, it wasn't raining when I left home, and we do have a garage, so I didn't get wet at all."

"Well, I'm glad to hear that. Neither did I have to go through the wet stuff, but it's raining pretty hard right now, and the lightening is terrible. Wondered if you'd like to come on over here and work during this violent weather? There seems to be the subject of ads that we need to discuss before you get your walking papers, right?" His deep masculine voice was quite sexy, yet she detected the humor. "May I send my chauffeur for you?"

"That would be nice." she admitted, thinking he was the only person in the world she would go out in that kind of weather for.

He said he would send a driver right over and they hung up. She wandered down the hall, running into Leona on her way back to her office, carrying a cup of coffee that was too full.

"Ain't it th' pits when I hafta get my own coffee these days?" she complained, with bottom lip jutted. "Bess usually has a cup on my desk but that gal's not doing a lot of things right lately. I think I'm going to have a talk with her."

"What's wrong with her?" Kutzie asked, as though she really cared. "Is she having some sort of problem or is it PMS?" She had taken an instant dislike to the woman that first day.

"If it is she has it every day of the month. She fumes and fusses about everything around here. Either she straightens up or she's history. Since you're working here now, I don't know if I need her any longer."

"She seems to think I'm responsible for a lot of things going on around here." Kutzie said bluntly. "She's hard to talk to."

"Well, she has emotional problems, Dear, so I try to overlook a lot of things she says or does, as everybody does around here." With that, she traipsed toward her office spilling the coffee, then she turned around and hollered back, "How's things going with the Hunt guy? Any closer to a deal?"

Kutzie could hardly believe the audacity of her boss yelling in such an uncouth manner!

She walked within close ear-shot of Leona before she answered quietly, "He's sending a car for me this morning so I won't have to drive in this weather. He wants to see other ideas, which I have in my briefcase."

They heard footsteps racing across the lobby and into the carpeted hall, and Bess, her face red from running, barged in exclaiming, "Oh, what a morning! Sorry I wasn't here on time to make the coffee this morning, Leona. I have such a terrible headache that I can't seem to shake and I'm just not functioning well."

"No prob," Leona said, and went into her office with a cigarette dangling from her bottom lip. Bess turned to Kutzie, "I suppose you're the one who made her coffee this morning?"

Kutzie simpered. "I hardly think so, Bess. I wouldn't think of competing with you in that department. Besides, I'm sure you make better coffee than I ever could."

Bess twisted her thin lips, and looking down her pointed nose with the small eyes slotted, snarled, "You are probably right about that. Well, you do your Hubbard's job, and I'll do my Elite job, and we'll get along just fine." She sniffed, and walked into Leona's office, and Kutzie walked away disliking Bess intensely.

Rusty's chauffeur came in for Kutzie soon after, and seconds later, she was riding in the limo to Hubbard's where Rusty was waiting. When the driver jumped out to open her door, Rusty had it opened already, and when he stepped inside and sat down beside Kutzie, he patted her arm, and winked. It excited her.

Brian slowly maneuvered the limo out onto the street, and in the heavy rain, and Kutzie glanced back at the huge store admiringly. She could hardly wait until she had enough money saved to go shopping there for the extra pieces of furniture she needed for her apartment.

Rusty took her hand. "Why are your hands so cold, Love? Is the car too cold?"

'Love'! I like that name coming from his lips. Aloud, she answered, "Just a little. The office was really too cold this morning, I suppose because of the dampness. I usually wear a light jacket when I'm there, but I forgot to bring one this morning."

He picked up his own jacket lying beside him, and wrapped

it around her shoulders before asking, "How's your mother?"

"I haven't heard any more. I assume she's about the same. I expected my father to call last night to tell me the results of the MRI tests, but I didn't hear from him. I plan to call him tonight. And, thank you for asking, Mister Hunt."

"There you go with that 'mister' stuff again. Tell me, Kutzie, do I look so old you want to call me 'mister' or what is it with you? I call you 'Kutzie,' I think you could call me 'Rusty'."

"I forget." she smiled. "It's not that I think of you as 'OLD'. It's simply respect for your position."

He smiled. "Thank you, my dear Kutzie. That's sweet, but call me Rusty, and I'll feed you. Now, what are you hungry for so I can tell Brian where to go?"

"I always enjoy chicken, of course, but most restaurants serve that, so wherever you decide will be fine with me." She wished she could name a fancy dish . . . something more sophisticated.

In minutes, Brian eased the limo to a stop in front of the Petite Auburge Restaurant on North Druid Hills road, and was out of the automobile in mere seconds opening the back doors, helping Kutzie out, and then Rusty. As they walked into the restaurant, all heads turned to stare at the striking young couple; the tall handsome man, and the beautiful petite, female companion on his arm.

The meal was enjoyable, the restaurant was extraordinaire'. Magnifique. The French cuisine was a new experience for Kutzie. From there they drove to Vinings Village which was in Cobb county. Rusty said he had some shopping to do; he needed to send a card to Chris, congratulating him on his engagement to Andrea.

Everywhere were signs that read 'Shop Like You Mean It'. And, they did. Kutzie had a wonderful time. Never had she seen so many boutiques, and Rusty was generous, buying her whatever she admired. She was so excited she wasn't sure if she should tell him not to buy the things, or if she should encourage it which the latter was her preference.

They entered the card shop, and began reading the humorous verses in the different cards, and the time passed quickly. They read the hilarious verses to each other, laughing until they cried. Rusty finally purchased one and from there they went to a candy kiosk located in front of the card shop, where Rusty bought chocolates. Kutzie teased him about eating again so soon after lunch, and he confessed that he was a chocoholic, and besides, the candy was his dessert and that made it fair. They walked along eating candy, and people-watching.

When Rusty saw the Coca-Cola store, he wanted to buy her a 'souvenir' compact, which she loved. Later, he carried all their shopping bags to the car while Kutzie stopped in at the Ladies room, and then met him at the car. Headed back to Elite, Kutzie's eyes danced when she told Rusty what a marvelous time she had. "It was all a 'First' with me," she confided, "my first experience with French food, and my first visit to the Galleria."

"Is that right?" he raised an eyebrow in that 'Clark Gable' way he had, and she sighed as she usually did.

They reminisced on their shopping trip as the rain pounded down so hard they could scarcely hear each other's words. Rusty sat as close to her as he possibly could as they remembered some of the silly, humorous verses they had read while in the card shop.

Rusty chuckled, "You're a lot of fun, Kutzie. I haven't been shopping in a long time. I usually let one of the girls do it all for me, because it never amounts to a lot anyway." Kutzie assumed 'one of the girls' meant an employee. Laying an arm around the back of the seat, and touching her shoulder with his fingers, he said, "Well, that was our work for today. It's almost time for you to get off work, but I want to keep you. I hate to let you go. But, I suppose you've got to report in to that ferocious boss-lady, don't you?" He touched her neck, and in little more than a whisper, said, "I can't wait to see you again, Kutzie. You're getting under my skin." She snuggled so close to him there was not even room for a thin sheet of paper between them as they drove back to her office. "To think I'm being paid for today, and it was the most fun day of my life," she murmured. "I don't believe we accomplished a whole lot of work, Rusty. Did we mention the word 'ad' even once?"

"Ad," he said, and they laughed giddily at the one word.

He walked her inside the building, and when he looked down at her and smiled, it seemed her heart would stop. "May we talk about more ads tomorrow?" he asked, winking in that unique way that was all his own.

She smiled and nodded. When she turned to thank him for the wonderful day, she saw that all heads were turned in her direction. She had amassed clout from her peers, because they all knew that he was Rusty Hunt, and she was the new girl that had performed the impossible feat of getting in to see Rusty Hunt, the invisible man. If only they all knew where she had gone to today.

Bess, standing in the hall, turned her head away as Kutzie passed her, snubbing her, about the time Leona walked up when she saw Kutzie arrive.

"Kutzie . . . I've been watching and waiting for you to return . . . I couldn't wait to find out how things went with Rusty Hunt today."

"We made progress Leona. We're getting there." Kutzie murmured, her head still in the clouds because she realized she was in love with Rusty Hunt! It didn't bother her because Bess had snubbed her, which was the way she wanted it. She didn't want to talk to that hell-cat anyway.

"Did you get far enough along to discuss any particular ads?" Leona asked, eyes stretched with anticipation.

"We didn't discuss anything in particular, no." Kutzie answered. "Just ads in general. He mentioned we should make a decision tomorrow."

"You're going back over there again tomorrow?" Bess asked. "How many times do you have to go over there to try to get an account?"

"And, what difference does it make?" Leona wanted to know, whirling around to stare into the woman's face.

"It's laughable that you think that he sees you as a woman, since he's only interested in men." Bess gloated, staring at Kutzie.

"What are you talking about?" Kutzie asked.

"You heard me. Rusty Hunt is gay. Everyone knows that." She was still gloating.

"I don't believe that!" Kutzie hissed. Right at that moment, she would've loved to slap her.

Leona, looking surprised as well as angry, asked, "I'd like to know how the hell you know about something like that?"

"I overheard some of his employees talking one day when I was sent over to talk with him about doing business with us. Some guy who went to school with him was the one talking about him."

Kutzie knew she was lying, but couldn't figure out why, unless it was jealousy. "What school?" she asked. "Was it here in Georgia?"

"Yeah, but I forgot which one he said, you know? He was saying that all through middle school, and high school Rusty made passes at him."

"Kutzie stated simply. "You know that's not true, Bess, Why are you lying?"

"Of course, it isn't true." Leona agreed. "And, don't you go around spreading rumors like that, Bess Henner. That man's too good-looking to prefer men over women."

"So was Rock Hudson." the woman answered coyly. "I know it's true, else why hasn't the man ever married as old as he is? He has to be forty if he's a day!" *I could tell you his age, but why waste my time*, Kutzie thought, and aloud, asked, "Did you talk to him at all the day you heard those lies?"

Bess squinted her small black eyes. "No! I told you he wouldn't see me! I went on to the coffee shop, and happened to mention to the waitress that the owner of Hubbard's was a real smart-ass, because he wouldn't even so much as discuss business with another company regarding the ads for the store. This man was sitting in the next booth, and he hollered over, and said,

‘Well, he ain’t interested in you because you’re the wrong gender, Lady.”

“I don’t want to hear anymore of this shit, ya hear?” Leona stated, gritting her teeth while glaring at Bess. “Just drop it right now. It’s a pack of lies.”

“I’ll ask Rusty tomorrow.” Kutzie said grimly. “He’ll tell me the truth.”

She had no intentions of forgetting it. She knew that Rusty never attended school in Georgia, but Bess, as dizzy as she was, may have misunderstood where he had attended school. As she pondered on the attention Rusty had lavished on her moments earlier, she knew it could not be true . . . it was a terrible lie. Rusty was a man who preferred women. She knew that. His interest in her was not one of pretense and besides, she had felt his manliness.

“You wouldn’t dare ask him a question such as that.” Bess hissed, and Kutzie simply smiled, “Oh, wouldn’t I? Honey, you don’t know me very well, do you? In fact, you don’t know me at all.” Bess’ small eyes widened somewhat, and she seemed a little nervous.

Chapter Four

The Stalker

When Kutzie briskly hurried from her parked car into her apartment that evening, she was startled by the movement of the azalea's near her front door. Someone was hidden behind the bushes! She hesitated a few seconds, then turned around, and went straight to the manager's office. Jan smiled a friendly smile when Kutzie walked in, but when she saw her facial expression, asked, "What in the world . . . ?"

"Jan, I've noticed several times this week that there's a man always hanging around my apartment. I also saw him at Elite today hidden in the garage. I've wondered if he works for you, although that doesn't even seem feasible since he came to my job site. I'm worried, and hoped perhaps you may know the man. He's out in front of my apartment right now."

Jan stood up, and reached for the front door keys. "Let's go see who he is. I'm curious. Sounds like a nut to me. What in the world was he doing?" she wondered.

"I think he may have been waiting for me." Kutzie said, tears spilling out the corners of her eyes because she was afraid.

"Have you told anyone else about this? Don't you think you should tell the police?" Jan asked, concerned.

"Probably. C'mon to my door with mc and let's see if he's still there." He wasn't. He was nowhere in sight. Kutzie thanked Jan for being there for her and Jan left to return to the office, assuring Kutzie she would try to find out if the person was an employee working on property for the owners, for reasons she was not aware of, or if he was a new resident. Kutzie wished Jan wouldn't go and leave her there alone, but of course never let on that she was frightened. *Get a grip, Girl! Don't let this dude turn you into a sissy and warp your mind.*

Kutzie went inside, making sure the front door was locked

securely, and answered her ringing phone. It was Ricky. She was happy to hear from him again. They talked awhile before she told him about the frightful man who kept cropping up wherever she happened to be. "What can I do?" she asked, worriedly.

"Unfortunately, Hon, not a lot. As long as he hasn't harmed you, the police can't touch him. If he hasn't done anything wrong, he can't be arrested. He isn't suspected of any crime, I suppose. Only thing I can tell you, Kutzie, is to be careful. Always be on guard."

"That's kind of scary, Ricky. A woman living alone being stalked by a big burly-looking man like that, and she can't do a thing to protect herself."

"Hey, I didn't say you can't do anything. You can buy yourself a gun, my dear. In fact, I strongly recommend it to anyone living in a large town like this or any other, because you never know who's going to do what."

"There must be another way, Ricky. Can't the police give a woman some sort of protection?"

He laughed. "Kutzie, my sweet. Don't be so naive. I say 'buy a gun', okay?"

"I may," she conceded. "But Ricky, I could never shoot another human being. I can hardly kill a bug."

"You will shoot somebody to protect yourself if you knew someone was about to harm you. It's simply a human nature trait. Please buy yourself a gun. You have a guy stalking you, looking at you with hate and snooping around your home. Buy a gun, okay?"

"What you say makes sense of course, but buying a gun in order to shoot a human being is inconceivable to me. Even using one to scare another human being is a terrible thought. Still . . . that guy does frighten me when he looks at me the way he does. I get a weird feeling whenever he comes around, and I know he is going to harm me if he ever gets the chance."

"See? You certainly don't want to wait until he's smothering you with a pillow, or choking the life out of you with a cord around your neck, and then start thinking you'd like to have a gun after all. Buy a little gun to carry with you to protect yourself from that son-of-a-bitch."

"But, Ricky, isn't it illegal to carry a gun without a permit?" she asked.

"We'll get you a permit," he answered.

"Will you go with me to show me the kind I need, then?" she asked glumly.

He assured her he would be glad to.

Next, she dialed her parents, and Amber answered the phone, elated to hear her sister's voice.

They were extremely close, despite the age difference. "Kootie," she squealed. "I was about to call you. We got the results of the MRI, and the doctor says Mom has something called 'Alzheimer's.' Do you know what that is?" Kutzie's heart fell when she heard the diagnosis. Exactly what she feared. "Sort of." she answered, distressed. "I've read some about it, and Rusty Hunt told me a little about it. What do the doctor's say we should expect?"

Amber cleared her throat. "They say it's a matter of time."

"The doctors don't think she'll get well? What does Dad think?"

"He says Mom will get better. But, Kutzie, he doesn't want to accept the horrible truth. He says the doctors are wrong. He's been acting so weird lately. I'm scared he's going to do something drastic. Please, Kutzie, come back home? Please?"

"Amber, Honey, I can't quit this job right now. I can't leave Elite hanging, and just come back home. I feel that it would be an injustice to walk out right now and leave Leona hanging. Besides, I need this job and we may ALL need for me to keep it. But, I'll be over to see you Sunday, Okay?"

"Koots, I really do need you! I need to talk to you . . . tell you things!"

Kutzie's heart went out to her little sister, but the real truth was that she could not walk out and leave Rusty Hunt, now that she had fallen for him. Or, maybe it was Bill. She couldn't bear the thought of leaving. She lived near enough so that she could drive over any time they needed her, and that had been one of the considerations regarding her accepting the Atlanta position. Amber could come to Atlanta to spend time with her, and could bring their mom and dad with her.

"Amber, let's talk about it when I come over on Sunday, shall we?" She was sorry, but she didn't wish to discuss the matter any further. "I guess we should hang up now, okay?" She was about to cry, for she was mourning inside for her mom. "Wait, Koots, I'm not finished. The doctor suggests a nursing home so she can receive the proper care."

"A nursing home? No way! I don't ever want her to go into a nursing home. We can take care of her just as she took care of us when we were children, and couldn't take care of ourselves."

"That's what Dad said, too. But, Kutzie, think about it. You're not even living at home to help anymore, and taking care of her is difficult. She can't talk, she doesn't know how to go to the potty any longer, she can't feed herself, she doesn't know what a glass of water is. She's really hard to handle. Shouldn't we at least consider a home so she can be cared for properly?"

"We can always take care of our mother, Amber. Let me talk to Dad a minute, please?"

When Richard said "hello", Kutzie scarcely recognized his voice. He sounded so tired!

"Dad? Is that you?"

"Hi, Baby. How's Atlanta and the new job treating my girl?"

"I love it here, Dad. I'm getting adjusted and learning about Atlanta. But you don't know how I miss you guys. I'm going to come over and visit y'all this next Sunday and spend the day."

"Well, there was never a question in my mind about your loving Atlanta. I can remember that you used to tell your mother and me when you were a little girl that you were going to live there one day, so I'm not at all surprised."

She laughed for the first time during the entire conversation. "I remember, Daddy. I think I'm still that little girl. Listen, Dad, I was just telling Amber, I'll be over to visit y'all this next weekend and I'll be there Sunday morning, about 5:30 or 6:00." She wasn't sure if she wanted to hear the bad word, "Alzheimer's," nor anything concerning a nursing home, which would lead to another depressing discussion. Why talk about it at all? They talked of other things for awhile, then she finally said, "Dad, Amber told me what the doctor said about Mom. Just take care of her, and I'll come over often to do what I can to help, okay?"

Richard assured her he would do that, adding, "Kutzie, we're worried about your mom, but we're going to learn all we can about the disease and she's going to remain right here at the house and get well, I don't care what those doctor's say." She caught the emotion in his voice, knowing that he himself did not believe his own words. "Anyway, you come on home to see us whenever you feel like it but don't think you have to baby-sit us, do you hear?"

Kutzie laughed again. "I know that. See ya Sunday. Love you." And, they hung up. And, she went to bed and cried herself to sleep.

When she awoke the next morning, she felt pretty good considering the emotional news she had heard the evening before. She ate a bowl of cereal for breakfast and left for work, her mind completely on Bill Davis as she walked to her car. She felt giddy and lighthearted, and happily singing a song, when a movement in the shrubbery startled her. She whirled around, and saw someone crouched behind it. It was the strange-looking man again and he started to run. She began to sweat as anger welled up inside her and her heart started to pound. She thought of chasing him down to ask what he wanted, always popping up like that. He was getting on her nerves and annoying her for sure. Why was he hanging around? She just might take Ricky's advice and buy herself a gun after all. Just remembering how the man had glared at her with those big white eyeballs with the small black pupils that reminded her of Satan, convinced her that perhaps she should purchase one, just in case. What could he want?

Again, the man ran away quickly when he saw her. She

didn't see where he went. She hoped to get a good look at the pickup he drove, so she could give the information to Jan, and she could find out if it belonged to one of the residents. How could such a big man run so fast and leave the scene so quickly? That was a puzzle in itself. She was depressed by then, and as she drove to work she no longer felt like singing.

* * *

Rusty was waiting for Kutzie in her office when she went in which surprised her. He seemed very glad to see her. She noticed that the other employees were gathered together in the doorway of their offices gawking again at Rusty Hunt as if he were a great football hero, or a movie star. The way they all stared at him with awe, and admiration, one could see he was just as important as any well-known celebrity.

She smiled at him while watching him smile his unique, one-sided smile with one raised eye-brow, as he rose and said, "I hope you don't mind my dropping by this morning to pick you up? I live fairly near here. I live in Buckhead. About a mile away."

Kutzie had heard that it was the elite section of town. She was about to say she was happy that he had, when Leona hurried in from her office when she heard his deep voice and didn't recognize it. When she saw the tall, handsome young man standing there, she knew he was Rusty Hunt for she had seen his picture in business magazines. In a loud voice she asked, "Wait a minute! Did I hear you say you came by to pick Kutzie up? Where are you taking Miss Kline? Is it business, or are you interested in her personally?"

Embarrassed at Leona's lack of tact, Kutzie put a hand over her face. *How could she say such a thing!*

But Rusty, being the gentleman that he must be, smiled ever so slightly, the eyebrow cocked, and as he gazed into Leona's red-rimmed eyes, standing with a cigarette dangling from the side of her mouth as smoke poured from her nostrils, said with mendacity, "You must be Leona Lutz, my dear, and you're as beautiful as I thought you would be. Kutzie has told me about her wonderful, understanding boss." He took her hand, and touched it to his lips.

Leona didn't move. She was as petrified stone staring at the hand he had kissed with eyes wide, mouth gaped and the cigarette stuck to her bottom lip, hanging there. Finally, with an emphasized broad smile he added, "I'm sure I will be interested in doing business with you, Miss Lutz. Miss Kline and I plan to talk over which ads to run today. She has wonderful ideas and those ideas were what sold me to your company in the first place."

Leona pursed her lips, assured him she was not worried about it, and flitted back into her office as Rusty wrapped Kutzie's arm in his, and walked her out to his white Town Car.

* * *

"There now, did you hear him say he's interested in HER when you asked him? No, you did not. Because he isn't. He's only interested in men, and that's why he didn't answer your question." Bess was smirking, egotistically. She tossed her head flippantly as they all watched Rusty and Kutzie walk out the door together, and get into the white Lincoln Town Car. Leona glared at Bess, turned on her heel, and walked into her office and slammed the door.

Bill, hearing a portion of what Bess said, walked over to her, and said, "Any man not interested in Kutzie has got to be nuts."

"Oh, the man's certainly not crazy. Only gay." Bess sniggered.

"Wha-a-t?" Bill seemed genuinely happy to hear that. "Do you know that for a fact?"

"It came from a pretty reliable source." Bess loved the attention she was getting at the moment from Bill. He usually ignored her.

"Who's the reliable source?" he asked.

"An old friend of Mr. Hunt's that used to go to school with him."

"All right!" Bill slapped his thigh, as he laughed heartily. "That's the best news I've heard in a long time. About as long as it's been since my last raise." He added that for Leona's benefit because even though her door was closed, he knew she had an ear against the door listening to every word that was being said out there in the hall.

Bess tossed her head, "Why? Because you're interested in him yourself?"

It was an arrogant remark to make, and Bill looked at her with disgust not bothering to answer. He simply walked off. Leona opened the door. "Bess, please come into my office."

* * *

Bill, buoyant over what Bess had said about Rusty Hunt being gay, almost sailed over to the water fountain where Treva stood. She was a cute little redhead with a smattering of freckles that everyone teased her about, always curious about what was going on. Bill gestured with both hands, saying, "Bess' trying to stir up trouble again looks like. Spreading rumors and gossiping. Leona's about to get her straightened out, I think."

"Hey, like go easy on the girl. She's like having problems at home. She found out a few days ago that her husband's like having an affair." She covered her mouth with both hands. "Oops . . ."

"Well, no wonder. Anyone would be easier to live with than that viper."

Treva, finished with her paper cup, tossed it into the waste basket and she strolled off, calling over her shoulder, "You oughtta be like ashamed. Well, I hafta like get back to my spreadsheets. Oh, and hey, like I haven't met the new girl yet but she sure is pretty, isn't she?"

"Kutzie? She's a doll. I'm trying to get to know her better myself. She's a little sweetheart."

"Whoa, whoa, whoa . . ." She stopped in her tracks. "I never like expected to hear that, old Mister Workaholic! Glad that somebody's like got your attention before you get too old."

He ran his hands through his blond hair and answered seriously, "I have to admit that I worry about her falling for that tycoon, Rusty Hunt. She's been with him almost constantly."

"Can you blame her? I could like go for him myself, only my old man wouldn't like it." She waved a hand, and walked off laughing.

* * *

"I can't believe you told Leona all that crap," Kutzie laughed. "I didn't know you were capable of such a snow job!"

"Hey now, the ol' gal's not so bad. But what's wrong with her mouth anyway?" Rusty grinned.

"She doesn't know how to apply lipstick. She wears too much and Lord only knows how she manages to get it all over her teeth and in the lines around her mouth." Kutzie giggled.

"That cigarette dangling like that got me," Rusty said, laughing with gusto. "I thought for sure all the skin was going to fall off her lips."

They laughed about the incident every time they thought about it, as they drove to Hubbard's with Kutzie nestled in the luxury of the white leather seats. Suddenly, because she was curious, she asked, "Rusty, how many cars do you own anyway?"

"Probably eighteen . . . nineteen . . ."

"You don't know?"

"Nineteen."

"What kinds?"

"Cadillacs, Lincolns, Rolls Royce, Mercedes, Lexus, Chryslers."

"My, my," she clicked her tongue, "So many! Which is your favorite?"

"I guess this one is. I'm a Lincoln man. What about you?"

"What? You're asking ME which cars I like? I'm no authority. I've only bought one car in my entire life and that's the Toyota I drive now."

He turned the corner onto Broad street, and as they approached the twin store buildings again Kutzie stared at the beautiful architectural workmanship of the enclosed bridge, realizing why he could afford so many cars. That store of his was truly the hub of Atlanta!

Rusty parked in the garage entrance, and he and Kutzie took an elevator up to his office.

She took some papers from her briefcase and handed them to him. He scanned them quickly and told her, "These are quite good, Kutzie. You're a very good artist. I like these. Have you studied art?"

"Yes, I took fashion designing. I thought I may choose that as a career once." She smiled.

"You could be a fashion model yourself." he said.

She thanked him modestly, dropping her eyes, wanting him to notice as her long lashes swept against her pink cheeks. When she looked up she found him staring at her with a strange look on his face. She wondered what he could be thinking. Did he admire her or feel sorry for her because she had tried so hard to keep her job? Perhaps he felt like her redeemer now that he was going to use Elite as his advertiser. Whatever he was thinking, he quickly changed from the sober expression she wondered about to a more cheerful one, and then they began talking, and continued to do so for hours on end about one little ad. Suddenly he picked up the ads and selected one to run the first Sunday in May as a Mother's Day Special.

Kutzie was taking in all the little things he said, the way he looked at her, the things he seemed interested in. "Yep, you could be a fashion model," he repeated, suddenly staring at her full lips. Again she thanked him, commenting that she always thought she would have to be taller if she were ever going to go into modeling. He laughed and raised an eyebrow. "You think so? Naw, you're the perfect size."

"Am I going to spend the day thanking you for the compliments you're paying?" she giggled. "Although, I really don't mind saying 'thank you'."

He laughed with her, and took her hand. "Let's go see Atlanta first, or would you rather drive to Dallas, Texas and see it?" She knew he had to be joking when he added, "I wish we did have time to spend a few days in Dallas. I really think you'd like it there. I miss my friends, especially our neighbors on Armstrong Drive, where we lived all my life."

Kutzie tried to keep from gawking like a country girl when they went to Peachtree Center. It was a 12-acre, multi-use development, in the middle of downtown. He took her into the

Apparel Mart, and the 3-level shopping center. They had a ball shopping for souvenirs and tee-shirts for families and friends. His arms were loaded with packages and he had to take them to the car and stash them in the trunk. When he returned they went to the CNN Center next. It was a 14-story megastructure composed of four free-standing buildings under one totally skylit roof! The 45 minute tour-walk was breathtaking. Besides, it was teeming with excitement. It was truly magnificent. The highlight for Kutzie was when they had an opportunity to witness the production of live news coverage.

Finally, they went to one of the restaurants, and had a bite of lunch.

"Where to now?" Rusty wanted to know afterwards. "Any place in particular you'd like to go?"

She dimpled prettily, "I have no idea where anything is in this town. All I know is that I love everything I've seen. It's been a fun-filled morning. I want to see everything there is in this city."

He seemed to enjoy seeing the sheer delight on her face. "Atta girl," he said with admiration.

"Do you think Atlanta is where you'll call 'home' from now on?" They were on their way out of the restaurant as they talked, and Rusty was holding her hand as he asked the question.

"Well, not necessarily. I haven't done much traveling, but I would love to. All I know for sure is that I don't want to spend the rest of my life in Charlotte, NC. I have life-long friends there yet, but most have moved away since graduation and it's not the same anymore. My sis, Amber, says she's going to move to Atlanta when she finishes high school, so I'll probably call this 'home' for several years anyway."

"She's not going to college? Amber, I mean?"

"Says she's not, but hopefully I can persuade her to when the time comes. This job with Elite would not have been possible without what little experience I had in advertising that I took in college." Kutzie still did not know why Leona Lutz chose her for the job assignment that she was on at that very moment.

Rusty paid the check, and they strolled over to the elevators while he held her hand again.

"I planned to take you to dinner tonight." Rusty said gingerly, as they stood waiting on an elevator. "I think you would like the Coach and Six Restaurant. I hope you haven't made plans?"

Because he seemed to be taking her for granted now, she answered flippantly. "Yes, I have made other plans for tonight. Perhaps we could go there tomorrow for lunch if you feel that you want to see more of my ideas then? Or are they opened during lunch? So many of the bigger restaurants aren't in Charlotte, but, of course, I don't know anything about this city."

"I don't remember if they're open for lunch or not but if they're not, I can have one of my girls call over there and I'm sure they won't mind opening for a little while during the noon hour." he said confidently.

"Do you mean businesses will open their doors for you if one of your secretary's simply calls to say you want to come in?" She asked overwhelmed.

He smiled and nodded.

"Are you bragging?" she laughed, and it seemed to embarrass him when she asked the question, no matter that he was kidding.

"Of course not. It's just that this is a dog-eat-dog world, unfortunately, and money can cause people to do strange things, and most businesses will keep longer hours for someone who pays for the service. That's all."

And then it was her turn to be embarrassed. "I was only teasing," she assured him wishing she had not taken the liberty to joke with a man she hardly knew. How presumptuous of her!

As he drove her back to Elite, her thoughts were on the fact that money could do so much and certainly could buy her mother the best medical care in the world. She felt that someone could cure her if they offered enough money. That was something to definitely think about . . .

As he walked her to the door she saw that the entire personnel was lined up again watching them, and she felt as though she were on parade. She strutted her stuff in her own sensuous way to give them something to really talk about, and she patted his hand as she told him good-bye when she went inside the building.

As she walked toward her office she saw Bess and Leona standing outside Leona's office in the hall with scowls on both their faces. She wondered what the problem was but had no intentions of getting in on their conversation. Aching to see Bill, she could hardly wait to see if he was in his office. Funny that she had fantasized briefly about what she and Bill could do if they had all of the money that Rusty Hunt seemed to have, while she rode in his luxurious automobile a little while ago. She strolled by his office nonchalantly, waving a hand at him as she passed before noticing that he was at his desk with his head down as if he were reading, and her heart skipped a beat when she glimpsed the thick shock of blond hair that was neat yet tousled, and an urge to run her fingers through it hit her. She considered sticking her head inside the door to say 'hi', but he seemed too busy to be disturbed, so she walked toward her own office telling herself to forget Bill Davis and concentrate on Rusty Hunt. A wealthy bachelor who was also good-looking was hard to come by, and mighty appealing to an average-income girl with a sick mother in need of costly medical treatment. So Rusty

Hunt was going to get her undivided attention from now on, and Bill Davis would be history other than only seeing him at Elite. But how could she resist Bill Davis' sweetness? He was already a dear friend and that meant a lot to her. Especially, since she didn't know many people in this town, and was very selective anyway about her friends. She felt comfortable with Bill and knew that he was her 'type'; honest, sincere, and upright. Little did she realize at that moment how her life would change in a matter of a short period of time.

The first thing I need to work out now, is how to GET mister Rich-guy. She suddenly realized that she had just turned down a date with THE Rusty Hunt. *Ye gods, what have I done? I'll never get him that way!* Well, they had already had a busy day and she simply wasn't in the mood to go anywhere else.

She enjoyed his company almost as much as Bill's, and they seemed to have a lot in common.

She had enjoyed the good times he had shown her so far more than she had enjoyed anything in a long time. Surely that meant she could enjoy being Mrs. Rusty Hunt. A checkbook with her name on it would be wonderful. Oh, yes . . . they were very compatible. The fact that Rusty could supply her with luxuries helped convince her that she could love him as much as she could love anybody. Even Bill. *What am I thinking? How can I even think of loving Bill? I don't know if I even LIKE him . . .* The more she thought about it, the more it seemed she was already in love with both of them, but wanting the one who could offer her the security she longed for was her priority for the time being anyway. Rusty was easy to look at, charming and easy to love, for she had already convinced herself of that. Bill was . . . well, he was . . . he was the sweetest person she had ever met in all her life, but dammit, she was not going to allow him to prevent her from having all that she had wished for all her life. Rusty was the answer to her dreams and she would have to be strong and not allow Bill to get under her skin. Their relationship must never develop into anything more than what it was at the moment . . . only friendship. So, that meant spending as much time as possible with Rusty and she simply would make it a point to avoid Bill whenever possible for they had to merely be friends. She doubted that they could really be close friends, without wanting each other. Many times during the past few days she had fantasized about what it would be like to be kissed by him. To kiss, and to eventually make love. Wasn't that a realistic dream? Of course it was. She was very confused. Where Bill was concerned she was weak and she knew it. He was captivating her every thought these days.

Saturday morning Kutzie slept in, finally climbing out of bed, yawning, after 10:00. She fixed herself a cup of instant coffee then called her father. She longed to discuss her mom's problem with him but soon found out that he didn't want to and wouldn't let her mention her name. He changed the subject every time. He kept repeating the same words over and over. "How are you? Are you doing all right?" And then he would ask her all over again.

"Sure Dad," she told him, almost afraid to acknowledge a difference in his attitude, and sensed that he was not well. She could not put her finger on what it was apart from the fact that he obviously did not remember that he had asked the same question already several times. It was exactly the way her mother had done about three of four years ago. He could not have Alzheimer's too, could he? What were the percentages of that happening in the same family when they were both too young to be stricken with the disease, or at least considered to be 'senile' in the first place? She was not sure what was considered to be the age that fell under 'aging' but she was sure the odds were against her father having the same problem.

She finally made him understand that she was fine and was for sure planning to drive over to visit the next weekend anyway, if she did not get over tomorrow as planned.

"I've been so very busy Dad, trying to get settled, that I haven't had time to get as much done as I would like to each day. Are you planning to spend this coming weekend there at home, or do you have something else planned?"

"Well, Amber's planning to go to the beach tomorrow with her new boyfriend. And, I'll spend the day here with your mother. We never go anywhere anymore. But, how about you? Are you okay?"

She sighed. "Yes Dad, I'm just fine. I just miss you guys. Amber has a new boyfriend?"

"We'll be over to see you soon." He obviously didn't even remember her question! "Your mom will be with us the next time because she's improving. Are you okay, Baby? How are you?"

She couldn't believe how he wasn't really talking to her. He didn't answer her questions, and he seemed to forget that he had already asked those same questions. Was he losing his hearing? Or his memory? Oh, God no, not his memory! Maybe she *should* go home tomorrow. She really didn't want to see her mother in such a bad way as she apparently was, but she couldn't avoid facing the fact that Melissa definitely was ill.

"Dad, did the doctor explain exactly what Alzheimer's is; what we should expect?"

"Well, yeah, but what do they know? She's fine. How are you though?"

She remembered at that moment, a listing of a telephone number she had noticed in the phone book regarding 'aging', which she planned to call, and Monday she would do that.

Kutzie was finding it hard to accept that her mother would never be well again.

She asked her father if she could speak to Amber.

"Hey, Kootie." Her sister's voice was cheerful. A welcome change from her father's sad depressing monotone one, even though she was sick of that stupid nickname that she had always called her by.

"I hear you have a new boyfriend. Tell me about him." Kutzie said joyfully. That was all she had to say, and Amber rambled on and on about Randy Green, a senior at the university, who was studying to become a veterinarian. Not once did she ask Kutzie if she were still planning to come over the next day. *What's wrong with everybody? Don't they love me anymore? Don't they care?* Kutzie was hurt, thinking no one missed her now that she had moved out. She told Amber she was happy for her, and they hung up and like all the other times after talking with her folks, she was down and feeling very depressed.

She sorted and washed clothes, took some to the cleaners, and later dressed for her date.

She wore a blue denim jumpsuit, red leather flats, and emptied her white handbag into a red one she planned to carry and last of all, stuffed a red handkerchief into the left breast pocket of her jumpsuit.

She drove to the mall where Margo's was having the shoe sale, but since it wasn't to start until 6:00, she shopped at other stores until time to go to Margo's, where she bought herself two lovely pairs of shoes, all the while keeping her thoughts on the dance. She was anxious to get to Studebaker's and to dance in Bill's arms. She could almost feel his muscular arms around her, and could almost hear the music, and she became almost lost in a fantasy world until the thought hit her that he may be the kind who danced apart from his partner. Heaven forbid! Please! She wanted to dance slow and have Bill hold her close in his strong arms. That was her fantasy.

Studebaker's was easy to find and a very nice place, she noticed. As she walked in she saw Bill waiting for her at the door. He took her arm, beaming with pride because she stood out in the crowd like a fashion model, with her long full auburn hair flowing about her shoulders and her pink cheeks flushed with excitement, and her eyes dancing.

Bill led her to a small table and their waitress, Nikki, a cute shapely brunette came by to get their order. They ordered only a sandwich. As they enjoyed the food, they discussed the day's events although it was not the subject either of them cared to talk about. When Nikki came by again they ordered a cocktail. Kutzie said sweetly, "I'd like a weak Lime Rickey."

"Honey, you don't have to tell them to weaken your drink

too much. They're very good but never too strong." Bill assured her. She wrinkled her nose and touched his chin playfully. "They might be too strong for me, so I always ask that they make them weak."

Nikki touched Kutzie's hair. "I love your hair. Is it naturally wavy or a perm?"

Kutzie thanked her and told her it was naturally curly, not a perm.

The first tune they danced to was slow and just as she had imagined, Kutzie fit into his arms perfectly. She loved it and while they were enjoying each other's company immensely, he suddenly became woozy and began to sway, then stumbled, trying to keep from falling.

"Whoa-a-," he said, "What's going on?" He seemed totally surprised, especially since he had not drank more than a sip.

"Bill! What in heaven's name is wrong with you anyway?" Kutzie asked, angrily. "Are you drunk? How many drinks have you had anyway?" Drunkenness was a definite turnoff for Kutzie.

He gripped her arm, holding on, shaking his head to clear it. "I haven't even drank *one* yet."

"Don't tell me that! What's wrong with you, Bill Davis, is that you're sloppy drunk and don't want to admit it." Kutzie was furious.

He struggled to walk naturally back to the table, but couldn't without her aid and holding on to the wall too. He sat on his chair, and sprawled trying hard to focus his eyes and trying desperately to tell Kutzie that something was wrong but his words were indistinct, and in disgust Kutzie picked up her purse, took her car keys out of it, and stormed out leaving him there to get home the best way he could.

Kutzie was so irate and disgusted with him, she didn't realize she had driven off in the wrong direction until less than a mile down the road, the car sputtered and finally it stopped running altogether. She couldn't see anything familiar. In fact, she could see nothing at all. Upon her arrival at Studebaker's earlier when it was barely dusk, reading street signs had not been a problem, but in the darkness where her car had stalled out she was unable to see any signs, much less read them. All she could see was darkness, and faint eerie flashes of light in the distance. She tried several times to start her car again and finally quit when it became apparent that she was running the battery down.

If only she could spot a telephone booth, she could call Triple A. She stepped out of her car shaking with fear, because she realized she was nowhere near civilization. Or, was she? She didn't have a clue as to where she was. She peered into the distance. Those eerie lights flickering could be a shopping center. Of course, a shopping center would have a telephone booth! She hurriedly pulled the straps of her handbag over her shoulder and walked toward the lights, believing she was almost out of her dilemma of being lost.

She walked rather slowly at first, but, as the force of her fear engulfed her, she got faster, faster. Something kept urging her on . . . go faster!

She had walked less than a block when she heard footsteps behind her. Afraid to turn around to see who it was, she hurried along her heart pounding, wondering what she should do. She had to keep going . . . no point in returning to her stalled car . . . She walked as fast as she possibly could thankful that she at least had on decent heels, rather than the high-heels she usually wore. Her legs felt like lead. She could scarcely move them. At least not nearly fast enough because she could tell that the footsteps were gaining on her! Closer . . . closer . . . She broke into a run.

Once she considered the possibility that it may not be someone following her at all but just someone out walking his dog. Certainly she had no reason to be afraid. But, when she carefully thought about it the idea seemed implausible! Of course it was someone definitely intending to catch up with her. She could tell. She couldn't look around, else it would slow her down and he would catch her. Lord only knows what he would to to her if he caught her!

Faster! She had to go faster! Why wouldn't her legs move? What was wrong?

Just ahead in the next block there appeared to be businesses. She saw dim store-front lights flickering. She hurried a little faster, with her chest heaving and throat dry. Once she twisted an ankle and faltered and stumbled, grabbing the air as she started to fall. But she didn't fall. She didn't know how she managed to regain her equilibrium, but she had a renewed zeal and she ran with all that she had left inside her. Then she approached the lighted area and discovered to her dismay, that all the businesses were closed for the night, which was only to be expected late at night had she thought about it!

Her breath came now in hard gasps. Her throat ached with pain. She stumbled on a piece of broken sidewalk and it hurt her foot.

Ahead were houses. They looked to be just across the next street. One had a porch-light burning faintly. Could she make it there before the man caught her? The footsteps behind her were gaining on her, and she couldn't seem to shake him! *If I could find a telephone, I could at least call a cab to take me home and I could come back tomorrow in daylight for the car.*

With renewed strength she bounded across the street, and bolted up on the front porch of the house where the porch-light was burning, and began pounding on the door! She strained her ears listening for the footsteps knowing they were right behind her. She was shocked when there were none. Where had he gone? She began to feel foolish then because there she was knocking on a stranger's door ready to tell someone that she was there because someone was chasing her. However, she still needed to find a telephone to get someone to come after her.

The person she thought was chasing her may have simply been on his way to one of the businesses, she decided. Probably a store-owner who had turned into his own business back there somewhere, while she was running from someone who probably had not even noticed her at all.

A woman's voice called from the other side of the door, "Yes? Who is it?"

"Please, I must talk to you." Kutzie called back. Perhaps the sound of another woman's voice may not be so frightening to the woman and she would open the door. She did. Slowly at first, and then a face peered out cautiously. Kutzie pulled on the screen door and found it locked.

"May I please use your telephone to call Triple A? My car broke down a few blocks up the street and I can't get it started." Kutzie said, talking as fast as she could before the woman slammed the door in her face. The elderly woman reached up, unlocked the screen door and let Kutzie come in. When she was safely inside Kutzie pushed the door closed quickly without a thought as to what the woman might think, although she didn't want to frighten her.

"The telephone's right there on that table." The woman nodded her head toward the table in a corner, eyes wide, staring at Kutzie as if she were a ghost. Kutzie fumbled through her purse trying to keep her hands from shaking so, and took out her wallet containing her AAA card. She dialed the number, gave the person on the other end of the line her membership number, then asked the woman, "Do you mind if I give them your address so they can send someone to pick me up to take me to my car?"

"It's 313 Sycamore Street." She was staring so hard Kutzie felt uncomfortable.

"They asked for the nearest cross street too. I'm sorry."

"Olive." The elderly woman continued to stare as if she knew Kutzie, and appeared frightened by her.

Kutzie placed the telephone back in its cradle, then with pleading eyes begging the woman not to put her outside, said, "I'm sorry I barged into your home like this but after my car stalled out and I started walking, someone was walking behind me and I was so frightened. I thought he was chasing me!"

Remembering her manners then, she offered her right hand, "Oh, by the way I'm Kutzie Kline. I got lost tonight because I'm new to Atlanta and haven't learned my way around."

The old woman shook it with her small scrawny one, saying, "I'm happy to meet you. My name is Annie. Please sit down." Kutzie sat on the edge of a tattered chair. "I'm very grateful you had your porch light on." she told the elderly woman.

"I leave it on whenever Junior is still out." The woman explained. "That boy! I never know where he is or when he's gonna decide to come home. He's a strange one, my boy is."

"How old is he?" Kutzie asked, thinking the woman was speaking of a teenager.

"He's thirty-eight but he ain't never cared 'bout nobody. He acts like he ain't got no heart or conscience or sumpin'. I think he's the white sheep of the family." She slapped her hands together laughing toothless. Suddenly, her face froze and she seemed much embarrassed. "Oh, I don't mean anything by what I said about his being a white sheep. I ain't calling no one a bad name, you understand?"

Kutzie could not understand why she would be embarrassed. "I know what you mean, Annie. We say a person is a black sheep because most sheep are white and a black one is a rarity. I think it's cute what you said and there was nothing wrong with it at all."

Annie stared into Kutzie's face, and asked seriously, "You say you've just moved to Atlanta? Do you have relatives here?"

"No, why do you ask?" Kutzie asked as she followed her into a small neat kitchen and sat on the chair Annie motioned to. Sitting felt good. She hadn't realized how tired she was. She had probably walked farther than she thought trying to escape from the man she thought was chasing her.

"Well, the judge that put Junior in prison looked exactly like you do." Annie told her, almost whispering. "I swear, the resemblance is unbelievable! But that was ten years ago and that woman would have to be in her forties now." Annie fussed with the cups and saucers as she talked and the noise she made rattling them around made Kutzie realize that her hands were shaking so, she surely was going to drop something.

"Junior worries me to death sometimes, Kutzie." Annie talked as if they were old friends.

"He's bought himself a red pickup truck, and where he got the money for it I don't know and how he buys the gas for it is beyond me. He don't work. It's hard for him to get a job since he can't talk. He don't have a tongue."

Of course she must have misunderstood Annie, Kutzie thought. "I beg your pardon?"

"He was in the wrong place at the wrong time talking to the wrong person. Anyway, a feller cut out his tongue. That was a long time ago. Junior cut up the man that did it pretty bad, and had to spend time in prison. He won't learn how to read and write so people can carry on a conversation with him . . . so he can communicate with people. It's hard. It's so hard . . ." Her voice trailed off and Kutzie was at a loss for words. She felt she should say something but all she could think of in response was: "Why wouldn't he want to learn how to write, to be able to converse and communicate?"

"He doesn't like anyone. He don't have no friends to talk to anyway, and I guess it don't matter if he talks to his mama or not." Annie seemed very sad.

The front door slammed just then with a bang. Annie jumped with a start, and Kutzie's heart began to pound when she heard the footsteps walking toward the kitchen. It was THOSE footsteps! The very footsteps that had followed her to Annie's house. Kutzie recognized them immediately. The same identical sounds that had echoed in her ears from the moment she left her car when it stalled. What was he going to do to her now? Was she trapped? The footsteps shuffled to the kitchen door and suddenly the curtain on the doorway jerked open so quickly both women were startled.

Kutzie thought she was going to die! Those large white eyeballs with the tiny satanic pupils were glaring down at her, as the large bulky figure hovered over her. Those eyes that she had seen in her nightmares. The weird-looking eyes which reminded her of the devil himself, so full of sheer hatred every time he looked at her. What Annie had just told her about her resemblance to the judge who sentenced him to prison had to explain why he had been stalking her. His mouth was curled into a vicious sneer that reminded her of a pit-bull-dog which was frightening to say the least. What was he going to do? Those few seconds were horrifying and Kutzie's life passed before her very eyes.

Annie's voice came through the fog of Kutzie's mind as she heard her say to her son, "Oh, there you are, Junior. I was wonderin' where you were and if you were comin' home t'night. We have a guest. Her name is Miss Kutzie Kline and she came to our door to ask to use our phone when her car broke down." He continued to stare with those evil eyes as he backed out of the room and disappeared. "That boy, that boy. I just don't understand him a'tall. He has no friends and don't want me to have none. He's always rude. I hope you don't think too bad of him for acting the way he did."

"Don't worry about it, Annie. A lot of people are shy like that. It's just the way they are." Her hands were clammy and her heart was literally skipping beats, but she kept her fear hidden from Annie because she could see that she was embarrassed by her son's behavior.

Kutzie was delighted when the doorbell rang. "I'll get it Annie. It has to be the wrecker coming for my car . . . and me!" It was. Kutzie thanked the hospitable Annie for her graciousness and hospitality and the driver helped her into the big truck. As she directed him to where she had left her car the driver asked, "What in the world are you doing in this part of town, Lady? It's bad over here and lots of bad things happen." Kutzie explained her circumstance.

Upon reaching her car, the driver said he'd like to check it out. "Just as I thought. Someone has deliberately pulled your distributor wires off. Happens all the time."

Lucky for Kutzie he was able to fix them. She shivered with fright at his grim discovery. Junior. It had to be Junior of course.

She followed him as he led her back to the freeway and from there she found her way home. Her little apartment never looked so good! She hurried inside, bolting the doors behind her even though she knew Junior was not out there on that particular night since she had just left him at his home.

Her teeth chattered yet her palms were sweating. She wedged a kitchen chair under the door knob, all the while fighting off a chill. *It's all Bill's fault! I hate him for what he did! A fine date he turned out to be!*

She checked the messages on her answering machine. Amber had called. Ricky had called. And Bill had called and he sounded so normal, not drunk at all! He didn't mention what time he had called, but asked where she had gone to and why she had ran out on him?

As if he didn't know!

She went to bed and had a miserable night sleeping. Not only did she toss and turn all night but every time she fell asleep she had a nightmare of Junior catching her and raping her, and she woke herself up at least twice, screaming and trembling with fright.

Sunday morning she crawled out of bed feeling as though a semi-truck had run over her, so tired as though she had not been to bed at all. But, sleep had been impossible because she kept seeing those tiny black pupils in the white eyeballs and the evil smirk on the fat oval face, that always reminded her of what the devil must look like.

She made herself a cup of instant coffee and the warmth of it helped some. Later, she took a blanket from off the shelf and curled up on the sofa and fell asleep, and rested a little while. The ringing of the telephone roused her from much-needed rest. It was Amber.

"Kutzie, I forgot you had a date last night when I called. We need to talk. I know you said you didn't want Mom to go into a nursing home but Dad's not able to keep taking care of her. I don't know what's wrong but he's not strong enough to care for her, and yet he thinks he is. She needs help now going to the bathroom and one of us has to do everything for her."

Kutzie interrupted her. "Amber. I haven't been gone from home long enough that Mom could have worsened so quickly. And Dad was fine when y'all brought my furniture to me wasn't he?"

"Not really. I think we've been so worried about Mom we just haven't been paying much attention to Dad, but he's not well. And he's changed. I don't know when because I just never noticed but he's different. He really is. And, Mom . . . she's so pathetic . . ." she started to cry. And Kutzie started crying also. The two young women held the telephone instruments to their ears, sobbing their hearts out when Kutzie heard her father's voice. "Kutzie, is that you? What are you girls talking about anyway that's so sad it's making Amber cry?"

Kutzie quickly straightened up and wiped her eyes and nose with a tissue from a box sitting on the sofa table. Forcing a laugh, she said, "Oh, Dad. You know how we girls act over silly movies."

He chuckled. "Yes, honey, I know how emotional you girls act over things you see in the movies or on television. I'm glad it's nothing more serious than that. Are you okay?"

"Of course I am, Dad. I just miss you guys a lot, but I'm doing fine here in Atlanta and staying busy. I hope to drive over to see y'all in a week or so." *Funny how she kept postponing a visit.*

"Good! I hope you can, baby. We miss you, too. Well, do you want to talk to Amber again? I think she went into the bathroom to wash her face."

"No, I think we finished our conversation. Tell her we'll talk later, okay? I love you. Tell Mom I said 'hello', and that I love her too."

She wasn't able to go back to sleep, because as always the conversation regarding the health of her mom depressed her so, but now Amber was beginning to act concerned over their father's health. Outside of his being somewhat forgetful lately she saw nothing wrong with his health. It seemed to her as if Amber was simply trying to find an excuse to lure her older sister back to Charlotte because she missed her. Kutzie smiled to herself at the thought realizing that she was missing them like crazy, but she also was going to stay in Atlanta and make Rusty Hunt propose to her so they wouldn't need to worry about the health of her parents so much. Besides she had to do something about this character Junior, who was stalking her. But what?

Chapter Five

Making It With Rusty Hunt

Kutzie dragged herself into the bathroom and took a warm shower. She had to start feeling better. As she stood under the warm stream of water she thought of Bill, puzzled by his message.

He was in such a condition when she left him she figured he would have to sleep it off a long time and yet he sounded as sober as anybody when he left the message.

The phone rang and she grabbed a towel and wrapped it around her torso, hurrying to answer it hoping it would be Bill again and she could ask him those questions. It was. When she heard his voice she became immediately incensed all over again but softened when she heard the concern in his voice. "Kutzie! What happened to you last night? I passed out for about an hour, more or less according to the security at Studebaker's. When I came to in the men's room, the office determined someone had slipped a mickey in my drink. I was worried about you."

"A mickey?" she repeated. "You acted dog-drunk Bill Davis, and I left you there!"

"Someone drugged my drink Kutzie, I swear to God I drank only half of that one drink. Don't you know I have more respect for you than to get drunk when we're on a date? Besides I don't drink enough to ever get intoxicated so when I started having that queasy feeling I couldn't figure out what was wrong. The security officer who determined something was in my drink took it to be analyzed. But why did you leave before you found out what was wrong with me?"

"Oh, come now Bill. You acted drunk so why should I stay around to see if you really were or not? I didn't know but what you may be an alcoholic, and did that kind of thing all the time."

She was somewhat ashamed now at leaving him, not believing him when he told her he had not drunk enough to be drunk. How could she have misjudged Bill's integrity and mistrusted him that way? She hardly knew what to say to him. "Bill, I'm sorry. I wish I hadn't left but I really thought you were drunk, and it hurt my dignity, I suppose. So much more happened last night!" Her breath caught just remembering.

"Why don't I come over, and you tell me about it?"

She considered her appearance, thinking, *I can't let him see me looking like this! If I look half as bad as I feel I'll surely scare him off because I must have bags under my eyes.*

"Give me a few minutes to get dressed, okay?"

* * *

When he arrived and she answered the door, she impulsively fell into his arms and began to sob. "Oh, Bill! Bill! It was so awful! I should never have left you. I'm so sorry I left you in the condition you were in because I feel like even that was my fault."

He looked down at her and smiled, "What? No way. Don't even think that for a minute."

"But, let me tell you about this big evil-looking man that's after me."

"A man is after you? Kutzie, what in the world are you talking about? Who's after you, for God's sake?"

"I started to tell you about this man showing up everywhere I went one day and didn't. He's been at Elite a couple of times and he seems to always be hanging out around my apartment."

She told him the story. When she finished he looked alarmed. "My god, Kutzie, the man has to be a lunatic. We have to do something. Let's call the police and tell them this story, want to?"

She shook her tousled mane for she had not taken the time to brush it before Bill arrived. "I have a friend who's a police officer. I told him about Junior the other day and he said they can't do anything until he actually commits a crime. I can put him under a peace bond but what good is a piece of paper? He suggested I buy myself a gun. That doesn't even make sense to me to buy a gun. I could never shoot an animal, much less a human being."

"Junior? A man is chasing you by the name of 'Junior'? The name makes me think of a little boy. But he sounds about as weird as they come, and we have to come up with something.

Then he squeezed her shoulders against him. "You're sweet, Kutzie, but you're in the real world here in Atlanta. But it's not only Atlanta, it's anywhere anymore. Even in Charlotte it's rough and dangerous, but you've never had to endure a situation like this before. If you're faced with the possibility that you may get hurt, you'll use a gun to instinctively protect yourself so I've been told."

"That's exactly what my friend said. But, I don't know . . ."

He led her to the sofa, and gently sat her down and he sat down beside her. "We need to talk about how we're going to handle this dude by the name of Junior. I tell you, that's the silliest name I ever heard especially for someone who looks as mean as you say he does. Does his mother know he's stalking you?"

"Oh no, Bill. I never would say anything to her about her son following me. She's such a sweet person and a wonderful mother, I could tell. It would hurt her too much to know I'm suspicious of her son stalking me. He's never really done anything to me, you know. I mean, he's just always THERE everywhere and the way he looks at me it's as though he hates the ground I walk on. That what's scary."

He nodded. "You're right. He hasn't laid a hand on you. Yet! But he's up to something. He's no doubt the one who slipped something into my drink! Why, Kutzie, is he after you, when he doesn't know you and neither do you know who he is?"

She told him what Annie said about her looking so much like the judge who had sentenced Junior to prison, and that she thought he must believe that she was that judge.

The two talked about every kind of different solutions they could come up with that may work although they were not actually solutions. Kutzie was not willing to discuss buying a gun to protect herself any longer, although she admitted to Bill that the day before she was seriously considering it.

Bill suggested she talk to her police friend once more and tell him what had happened the night before and see what his thoughts were on that.

He stood up and pulled her to her feet. "Let's go get a bite to eat somewhere, want to? You'll feel better and so will I. Have you eaten anything today?"

She had to think about it, before she shook her head. Then laughing, she said, "Seems like we're always eating. I'm glad you live close by, Bill. I don't know how I could function with this problem without you to talk to."

He put an arm around her and kissed her cheek. "I'm glad you live close enough so that we can at least go out to eat during the weekend. Remember, I told you how I hate to eat alone?"

They walked out to his Lexus and they enjoyed another meal together.

Kutzie had a pang of guilt once in awhile throughout the meal realizing that Bill was a far better person than she had given him credit for. He had higher morals than she realized when she walked out on him the night before. She wanted him to know she was sorry but she didn't know how to convince him. She told him more than once and still it did not seem adequate.

"Bill, would you like to go back to my apartment so we can talk awhile longer about what you think I should do about that Junior person?"

"Well, if the police can't do anything with him until he hurts you in some manner, or kills you, heaven forbid, I'll kill him first before he'd ever get a chance to get to you and harm you in any way. Obviously he's a creep, 'cause there's not a doubt in my mind that he drugged me, tore the wires off your distributor and there's no telling what else he'll try. We have to stop him!"

"Don't you want to come to my apartment to talk more about it?"

He was surprised, that was obvious. Smiling, he said, "I thought that's what we were doing. Are you saying you're ready to go? You're done eating?"

She nodded.

"Anywhere else you've decided you'd like to go while we're out? It's such a beautiful day it's a shame to waste it."

"I think I'd rather go home." Her voice was merely a whisper.

"Well, we're not going to be wasting it since I'm with you because time with you is never wasted and always cherished," he said as he shrugged his wide shoulders, paid the check, took her arm, and they walked out to his car. Gently he helped her in as though she were a fragile doll.

All the way home they seldom said a word other than to discuss the dogwoods and the other trees, and how the flowers had bloomed so beautifully. Kutzie was unusually quiet.

When they walked inside her living room she sat down on the sofa and patted the space beside her, indicating that she wanted Bill to sit beside her. He did and turned to look at her, obviously wondering why she was acting so strange. "Anything wrong?" he asked.

Picking a loose thread on the sofa cushion, almost shyly she said, "I feel so bad about misjudging you, Bill. I never knew how much I've learned to care for you during these few days since we met. I think I love you." She hadn't meant to say that. The words seemed to pop out of her mouth before she could stop them. However, she thought to herself, she could have said that she KNEW she loved him . . .

His hazel eyes widened, and he looked as though he had been hit with a bolt of lightning! He held her hand stroking it without realizing that he was doing it and finally, clearing his throat, he looked straight into his eyes. "Kutzie, don't tell me this unless you mean it. You don't know how I've wanted to hear you say these words but don't joke about it."

"I'm not joking. I do love you."

Tenderly, he loosened his fingers from hers and slipped an arm around her shoulder and pulled her toward him, then tilted her chin so he could kiss her full lips, only lightly at first then hungrily as he held her tighter, and the kiss became more passionate. When he lifted his head only inches away from hers, me murmured, "You're so sweet, Kutzie. I think I love you more than I need to."

She didn't want to hear the word 'think' . . . She wanted to hear it as fact!

She did not say anything, she simply wrapped her arm around his neck and pulled his face down to hers and kissed him quite intimately. And, again. And, again.

Abruptly, he pulled away and stood up, and began pacing the floor. Running his fingers through his hair, he seemed stricken. "What am I doing? I can't believe I was thinking of doing something I would only regret later."

"What?" she asked innocently, eyes wide, sparkling with desire.

"I feel like I'm about to take advantage of you." He dropped beside her again and took both her hands in his big strong ones. "Sweetheart, I think too much of you to take advantage of a situation. Don't you see? You're trying to convince me that you're truly sorry about last night but this is not the way to do it. I don't want you hating me tomorrow for what we did today because you're feeling you should make amends. I don't play that way even though I would love to make love to you. You're sweet and I respect you, but I also love you. A lot!"

She loved him all the more when he said those words to her and she realized his morals were even higher than she had given him credit for. She smiled at him, and patting him on the face whispered, "Thank you, Bill, that's sweet of you to say that. Kiss me again only just a little gentle one this time, okay?" And, he did.

He didn't stay much longer, because it was Sunday and he had chores to do around his apartment. One thing Kutzie had noticed about his place was that he kept it extremely clean. She had once assumed that bachelors live like pigs though she had no reasons to back up her fallacy since she had never been inside a bachelor's home before Bill's.

He gave her a quick peck on the cheek and went home.

Monday morning, they greeted each other in a business-like professional way, but there was a special bond between them. Kutzie could hardly believe what tremendous moral strength he possessed, for his self-control was beyond belief especially since all the men she had dated in the past had been young animals, always hot to trot.

She felt more adult Monday morning than she had on Sunday when she had a chance to realize she must have sounded much like a teenager might the night before.

Leona walked into Kutzie's office, saying, "You look like the cat that ate the canary."

"Why?" Kutzie asked wondering why she said that.

"Oh, I dunno. Thought maybe you had your mind on Rusty Hunt, that stinkin' charmer. Are you expected over there at his office again this morning?"

"I guess I should call him?" Kutzie stated with a slight chuckle at what Leona said.

When Rusty's secretary buzzed his office, Rusty greeted her in that deep masculine voice. "Kutzie, I was about to call you. Are you going to drive over or shall Brian and I pick you up?"

"I'll drive over. Any particular time?"

"The sooner the better, of course."

"Of course. I'll be right over."

Leona lit a cigarette while Kutzie talked to Rusty on the phone and Kutzie wondered how she could dangle it from her bottom lip, even as she said, "Good deal, gal. I'm anxious for you to get this settled and let's get those ads in the papers and magazines ASAP. Hopefully, you can get an idea of all he expects us to do for him as far as the advertising types, campaigns, and so forth."

Kutzie nodded. "I'll do all I can to light a fire under him."

"Well, be careful about the kind of fire you may be lighting," Leona snickered. Kutzie laughed and reached for her handbag. She took her car keys out of it, saying as she walked out the door, "Wish me luck, Leona. I'll be back as soon as we make some decisions."

She walked by Bill's office, and when he looked up he winked, and she puckered her lips at him . . .

Rusty was waiting near the escalator which amused her to see him there. "Why are you out here among other human beings?" she teased, sure that he was merely waiting for her.

He grinned, with a twinkle in his eyes. "I love 'em all. That's where my money comes from."

"Mine, too." she smiled, "So shall we go to work?"

"Work?" He echoed, slapping a palm over his eyes. "Oh, no! I avoid that word whenever I can, but under the circumstances may be I can handle it since a beautiful girl is going to be working with me." They were walking toward the corporate offices as he spoke.

"Really? Who?" she asked and they both bellowed with laughter. She enjoyed their times they had together for they seemed to always laugh at the silliest things.

"Where are we going for lunch today?" he asked, looking up from the papers she handed him.

"Rusty! All we ever do is eat!"

"We have to eat in order to think clearly. Here's the ads I

want Elite to start working on for this coming month so our work is out of the way for today. It's all in there and all you need to do is to hand it to Leona and she'll think we worked on it all day today."

Kutzie hit his arm. "You devil you."

They went to lunch at 'The Wild Ox', and ordered filets. They thought about having a glass of wine but both changed their minds because they were on the job. Kutzie would worry if she were to drink one little glass because sometimes wine affected her and made her woozy, when other times it did not but usually white wines were what bothered her.

They were in the restaurant two hours and when they left arm in arm he drove to the zoo, and they walked around laughing at all the silly antics of the animals. Kutzie loved the monkeys and Rusty enjoyed the lions and tigers. He said they reminded him of himself and Kutzie roared with laughter. They ate popcorn, corny dogs, and drank cokes all afternoon.

Around 4:00, they left, and Rusty rushed her back to Elite, so that she could give the ad work to Leona to make her day, and besides Kutzie got off work at 4:30. She almost forgot about her date with Ricky that night and when she arrived home she hurried to change her clothes. She wanted to wear something comfortable and since they were only going to a movie, she wore her newest jeans and a turquoise cotton sweater.

Ricky looked handsome in his tan Dockers and black shirt. She thought he had looked good in his uniform but he looked super in ordinary clothes. She was proud to walk into the theater by his side and he beamed with pride when he looked at her.

She was already beginning to feel a little uncomfortable because of all the junk food she had eaten that day and couldn't eat the popcorn he bought. She sat beside him listening to him eat the popcorn while she was feeling more and more nauseated. When they stopped at a small cafe after the movie, she had a chicken sandwich because she felt she needed something solid inside her tummy, but later she wished she hadn't. She was really suffering with a stomach ache by then and she wanted to go home and take some medicine and go to bed.

She thanked Ricky for a wonderful time apologizing because she felt so terrible and had to go home early. The date he had probably looked forward to, was ending too early in the evening to suit him, Kutzie saw by the expression on his face. When he asked for another date she asked him to call her later in the week. She didn't want to discuss anything at that time. She wondered why she wasn't interested in him anymore? Why did she wish she were with Bill instead when she was feeling so sick?

She knew she needed to take something to ease her upset stomach. A party-pooper she was not but she was sick and nothing but relief seemed important to her. She seldom had a tummy ache, but she had never spent the day at the zoo eating all the junk food they sold either.

When he walked her to the door, Ricky looked as if he were expecting a kiss, but Kutzie hurried inside when he had unlocked the door saying, "Ricky, I'm sorry that of all nights I'm not feeling well but, we'll have fun next time, won't we? I usually never get sick, but . . . it's just one of those things."

He half-way grinned, and kissing the top of her head assured her everything was a-okay and left. She hurried to the bathroom for the Pepto-Bismol and that was when she heard a sound from another room. Frightened, she tiptoed toward it listening intently, trying to determine what it was as she stealthily crept along. She heard it again and because it was in the quiet of the night she could hear the person breathing! It was so dark she could not see even an outline of anything and the hallway was too dark for her to be seen either. She was thankful that she had thought to turn off the bathroom light upon hearing the noise. She tried to remember where she had placed certain items of furniture so she could slip into the living room without bumping into anything and see if she could determine where the burglar might be hiding. Her thoughts were racing as fast as her heart was pounding as she wondered what she would do if she were to suddenly be looking the person in the eye? She would simply die! He had to hear the pounding of her heart and her shallow breathing, or at least hear her gulping air like a guppie.

She felt along the wall taking one slow step at a time, until she bumped into a little table she had sitting against the wall with a glass clock sitting on it. When the clock fell to the floor and shattered, the noise echoed in the quiet of the night and was deafening!

She heard someone running, and then the slam of the front door. Switching on the hall light, she scampered through the apartment and found the front door standing wide open but no one was in sight. She stood there frightened and shaking as she had done too many times recently, and drained of all energy she walked slowly into the bathroom, leaned over the commode and spilled her guts out. She felt faint and lowered the lid and sat down. After a moment, she washed her face with cool water and walked back into the living room wishing for her mom. She thought of calling her father to let him know what was going on but what would be the point of that? What could he do? After all he wasn't next door to her!

She called Bill.

In five minutes he was by her side. He held her tightly as she cried telling him everything that had taken place during the day. She could see that he was upset about her being at the zoo all day long with Rusty, much less eating junk food that made her sick. He frowned but didn't say a word except, "There,

there, you'll feel better tomorrow and don't worry your pretty little head about things. Before I leave here tonight I'm going to find out how someone was able to get inside your apartment. Do you think it was that Junior?"

She raised her head from his shoulder. "Who else but? Bill, who is he? Why can't he leave me alone?"

"The man must be a psycho. I don't want to frighten you, Sweetie, but we have to be realistic. Those kind of people are very dangerous. They do these things to get their kicks. We need to see what we can do about the buzzard. By golly damn, I'm not going to sit around and let him harm you before we do something to stop him!"

She smiled at him feeling very protected. He pushed her hair back from her forehead, then rose and went from window to window inspecting each one carefully. He finally stopped at one, and said, "Kutzie, this window apparently was not locked and he came through it to enter your apartment." She jumped up off the sofa and ran to see the one he was talking about. She thought she had checked them all when she first moved in. She put a hand over her mouth when she saw it, wondering how she could have possibly been so careless.

"It beats me how a man as big as you say Junior is, could climb through here but he must know how to squirm through like the snake he is." Bill replied grimly. He locked it securely and took Kutzie by the hand and they walked back into the living room. "I hate to leave you alone but I guess I must. Is there anything else I can do before I go?" he asked gently.

"Bill, I don't want you to go. Could you spend the night? This is a very comfortable sofa for sleeping." Her green eyes were limpid and pleading, and bottom lip puckered. He shifted first to one leg and then the other, and looked at her, helpless and undecided. He probably would do anything in the world for her but he asked Kutzie what would her neighbors think if they should find out she had a man spending the night with her? She whispered, "I don't care what the neighbors think." He pondered on it a moment then grinning boyishly, he suddenly asked, "Want to go with me to my apartment to get a pair of pajamas and something to wear to work tomorrow?"

She did. They walked out to his car and he opened the passenger door and helped her in.

At his apartment she waited in the car.

Her place was less than a minute away from his and as he parked in a space near her apartment Kutzie gasped, "Look Bill. That man is standing beside my bedroom window. It's Junior again!"

Bill bolted from the car and took off running toward the direction she had pointed, but Junior undoubtedly heard the car door slam and he was off like a streak into the blackness of the night.

Bill chased him about a block, but the man disappeared into the inky blackness of the night and he gave up, and returned to Kutzie's side. He took her arm and they walked into her apartment. He was trying to steady her for she was shaking so. Finally, he held her in his arms until she calmed down.

"It looks like you're going to have to buy a gun after all, to scare that sorry bastard into leaving you alone."

Kutzie closed her bedroom door and readied herself for bed. She felt content and relaxed knowing that Bill was just in the next room ready to protect her should Junior return again that night.

But what about the next night? And the next and the next? She lay awake worrying about that for a long time, finally dropping off to sleep well after midnight.

Junior did not come back that night because undoubtedly he saw that she was in the company of a man. Kutzie and Bill worked out their schedule pretty well as far as the one bath usage went.

The next morning he was dressed and making coffee out in the kitchen when she awoke and began to get dressed. She applied her make-up in the bathroom and put on her dress while standing inside her closet, except for her stockings which she donned while sitting on the side of her bed.

The coffee smelled delicious, and she walked into the kitchen and saw that he had a cup of coffee poured for her already. She smiled her sexiest smile, "This is great! I think I'll keep you."

He winked and smiled. "All right! I'm making toast. I hope you don't mind my taking over your kitchen like this but hey, I do this sort of thing every morning. Can't get lazy just because I spent the night with my girl."

They both laughed at his remark. "No one would believe you slept on the sofa and that we behaved ourselves, would they?" Kutzie wrinkled her nose as she said it.

"We won't tell anyone just to test them will we?" Bill asked, jokingly. "Shall we ride to work together in my car?"

"I think I'm going to have to drive back over to Hubbard's again today, so I guess not but we might consider car-pooling once we settle Hubbard's account."

"I wish it were settled now. I hate you're spending so much time with that rich tycoon."

"Why, Bill, I think you're jealous."

"I am. I'm jealous of all that he can give you and I can't, and it would be selfish if I . . ."

"Bill. Listen. I'm not interested in what he can give me. I disliked the man at first, but I've gotten to know him well enough to know that he's a fantastic person. We may go out together once in awhile because, why not? Neither of have any commitments . . . not going steady or anything, certainly not engaged to anyone else. And it's a great way to get to know people in this town, being seen with him I mean. Like over there at Elite . . . whenever he brings me back from the store the entire staff is standing near the door watching us. I've seen all of the employees right there at the entrance." She watched his expression as she made up excuses regarding her relationship with Rusty Hunt. She knew she wasn't making sense when she attempted to explain to Bill why she wanted to continue to see Rusty but she couldn't tell him the real reason. Only she would ever know why. Anyway, she was in love with both of them, she realized. In love with both Rusty and Bill, and didn't want to give up either of them.

* * *

Sure enough, she had to leave to go to the department store almost as soon as she arrived at work. Rusty had left word with Leona that he was going to be in the store at 9:30 that morning and would be waiting for Kutzie at the side entrance to let her into the store before it opened at 10:00.

As she approached the door he was there pushing it open for her, grinning broadly. "How are you after our wild day yesterday?"

"What a tummy ache I had," she confessed. "Did all that junk food affect you at all?"

"No, not at all. I really didn't think we'd eaten all that much. Especially you. I betcha you didn't eat more than a half-plate-full, if it had been served all at once on a plate." He put an arm around her shoulder, "I am sorry it made you sick however. Were you real sick?"

"Pretty much. Well, I just felt crummy. I had a date and I was dull and boring while we were out."

"Good!" he commented.

"Good?" she echoed.

"Because you were dull and boring on your date. I'm truly sorry you didn't feel well."

"It surprises me that you should care one way or the other," she retorted.

"I'm jealous that's all. I envy whomever you were out with."

"But, why? That doesn't make sense to me that you would care if I go out, or not."

"I've fallen for you, Woman. Don't you know that?" He attempted to make light of his words but his eyes told her he was quite serious for he looked longingly at her. Kutzie was thrilled. At that moment he was the most important human being in the entire world, and she longed to melt into his arms. But how could she reveal her emotions right there? She simply laughed, as though it were all a joke and asked, "Why did you want me to come over so early this morning?"

Suddenly he pulled her into his arms. "Why do you think I asked you to meet me here before the store opened, Kutzie? I had to have some time with you to let you know I have fallen madly in love with you. I've never known a girl quite like you and you're all I can think of day and night. I had to find out how you feel and there's always people around. Except now in this empty store. Is there any chance at all that you can learn to love me also?"

She raised her face to look into his eyes and she scanned the handsome features. The firm jaw-line, the dark hair that always had a loose wisp partially fallen on his forehead, the dark mustache, the deep dimple in his right cheek, and the deep cleft in his chin. She tried to devour it all right then right there! He held her head and kissed her lips. Slipping both arms around his neck she kissed him back, and they held each other tighter and tighter. The kisses became more passionate and before she realized it he picked her up in his arms and carried her to the elevator, and into his office where he locked the door as they continued to kiss each other the entire distance. He placed her tenderly on the huge settee in the foyer of his office and lay down beside her . . .

It was after 10:00 when Kutzie bubbled, "Oh, my gosh, the store's opened. What do I do now? I can't go out there looking like this. My clothes are all wrinkled where I dropped them on the floor." She held up the silk blouse she had worn. "Look at this!"

Rusty laughed while stuffing his shirt-tail back into his trousers, and fastening his belt. "I'll run over to the ladies' department, and bring you something to wear. What size?" And, he leaned over to kiss her.

"Size thirty-four blouse." She answered.

Because she was stark naked, she took his jacket from the coat rack and put it on as he slipped out the door with head held high, feigning confidence. He looked as nice and wrinkle-free as he had when she first saw him that morning she noticed, while hers looked like the cheap clothes that they were because they came from a discount store.

When he brought the shirt, he also brought a pair of slacks back to her. "Can you wear a size five?"

She nodded. "How'd you know that?"

He smiled. "I didn't. The saleslady said she wears a seven, so I figured it out, and brought the next smallest size."

"You're a genius is what you are. You asked her what size she wore?" Kutzie laughed.

"Well, I said they were for my mother, and that they were

about the same size. That part was true but she didn't know I chose a smaller size because I wasn't getting them for my mother."

Kutzie stepped inside the supplies room and got dressed. The new clothes fit perfectly and she loved his good taste. She felt the silk material of the pants and realized they felt much differently then her silk blouse that had wrinkled so. That surprised her. She was not an authority on fabrics, and had never been one to spend money on expensive clothes. Most of her clothing came from discount stores and sales racks.

Rusty wrapped both arms around her, whispering, "Kutzie, darling, I never meant for that to happen, believe me. I couldn't seem to think about what was right and wrong because you have me so completely under your spell and whatever we do has to be right. I fell in love with you that first day when you came into my office so completely fresh and innocent. I want you to marry me, my darling."

"Rusty, I was told that you're gay and even though I didn't believe it for a minute I guess it was natural for me to wonder about it. I suppose that was why I allowed you to go all the way. I had to know. Yes, I'll marry you because I fell in love with you that first day, also."

He scanned her face. "What are we supposed to do now? I wish I could take off work and we could make wedding plans but I've already taken off work so many times the past few days I'm getting behind in everything. I want to tell my parents and my brother, and I know you want your family to know. Can you decide on the wedding date and handle whatever you need to do by yourself today? Do you need some money?" He pulled a wad of bills from his pocket and she took them, smiling, then tickling him under his chin and wrinkling her straight little nose, said, "Calm down. I'll take care of everything. When you get off work this evening we'll call both our parents if you can remember where yours are this week. And, we'll call Chris and your Uncle Nick."

Stooping to kiss the tip of her nose, he whispered, "I think I have pretty good taste. You should see how sexy you look in that new outfit."

"I feel sexy, too. Look what I'm doing right now." And, she stood on tiptoe and kissed him.

She drove back to Elite and walked straight into Bess' office, and she was the one who now did the sneering. "Just thought it might disappoint you to know this, but Rusty Hunt ain't gay! He proved that to me awhile ago."

Bess' mouth dropped open and Kutzie turned and walked out the door. She got a kick out of letting her know he wasn't gay, but she didn't bother to tell her the good news of their engagement. She wanted Bill to be the first to know. When she walked into his office he whistled when he saw her. "Wow, you look cute, little doll."

"Thank you very much." She looked down at her nails and shifted her feet. "I came in to tell you something Bill . . . Uh, . . . Rusty proposed today."

He raised an eyebrow. "Why does that not surprise me? If anyone can get him you can."

She stood there gaping at his handsome features, wanting to take him in her arms and hold him close. He looked so sweet sitting there. But then she had to watch that handsome face crumble to pieces the next moment, when she continued, "And Bill I accepted."

He stood up dropping both arms to his sides saying nothing. He just stared at her looking so hurt. She thought he was going to cry. And that she was also. Then he smiled a slight one-sided hint of a smile. "Well, well, congratulations, Kutzie. I want you to know that all I want is your happiness. Seems like this happened awfully fast didn't it? Have you set a date yet?"

"We're going to notify his family and mine tonight and then we'll decide when. And yes I suppose it did happen awfully fast."

"Well, too bad the rumor Bess was spreading isn't true. I hoped it was Kutzie, really. For what it's worth you know I told you I'm in love with you myself and I meant that sincerely. So, if it doesn't work out for any reason I'll be waiting for you, okay? I mean that."

She fell into his arms. "Oh, Bill it's so confusing to be in love with both of you at the same time! You have no idea how I'm pulled between loving you as I do and loving Rusty also."

"Wha-a-t-t? How can you say that to me after telling me you accepted Hunt's proposal, and how can you even think of marrying ol' Rich-y boy if you love me?" he was without a doubt puzzled, and hurt.

"I told you. Because I love you both and he proposed first." She laughed lightly, teasingly.

When he looked at her as if he was not sure he comprehended, she continued, "I do love him and it's all I should have said. Sorry."

Darling, it's hard to explain that it's not too hard to love a millionaire, though I love you . . . really love you. His eyes disputing he stated simply, "No, you don't," as if he had read her thoughts, and he clenched and unclenched his fists and his jaw tightened. And, when he said that she raced from his office into her own, and closed the door behind her. She was shaking so hard, she dropped into her chair fighting to keep from bursting into tears. Why was she so upset, when she should be happy beyond words. An hour ago she had been walking on air, and now the bubble had burst and she was in the depths of despair.

She opened her handbag, and took out a powder puff and patted her nose with it. No one must see her crying. Why, this was the happiest moment of her life!

When her telephone rang, startling her back to reality it was Rusty. "How are you doing, Sweetheart?" he greeted. "I've been going like a house afire since you left trying to play catch-up around here so we can do whatever we need to do to get started on those wedding plans of ours. Why don't we simply elope, and tell all our family and friends after we return?"

His voice lifted her spirits so she was back on Cloud Nine.

"We don't want to disappoint everyone by eloping, do we?" she giggled.

"I don't know why not. I never proposed to a girl before so I have cold feet."

"Hey, Mister, what about me? I never accepted a proposal before and this is also new to me. And, guess what? I've never been a bride before either." They laughed hilariously.

"Can I pick you up in a few minutes? I'd like to call my parents and when I talk with them I want you beside me."

"I'll have to ask Leona unless you can wait until after I get off this evening?"

"Darling, you can tell that woman to buzz off forever, if you want to. You'll never have to work again. If you want Elite I'll buy it for you." She could almost see that crooked smile on his lips as he talked, which she loved.

"Rusty, we're not married yet." she reminded him, "I have to work and support myself for awhile longer because I don't want Elite and its headaches."

"No, you don't have to work. You can move in with me today and allow me to start taking care of you."

"But, I just signed a lease. I can't just move out." *Neither will I move in with you, dear boy.*

"Sure you can. We'll pay off the balance of your lease. That's all they want."

"I can't do that. I can't move in with you until we're married. What happened today can't happen again Rusty, until after we're married. Okay? I wasn't myself this morning."

"Hey, Darling, whoever you were I loved you. Whatever you say. I'll pick you up shortly."

He made a smacking sound as if he were kissing her, and they hung up. When she turned Bess was standing there. "What do you want?" Kutzie asked, curtly.

"Just listening. I guess you did prove that he's not gay, unless he likes both sexes? There's lots of people like that too, you know."

"Bess, please bug off and leave me alone. I think you have a warped mind. We have nothing to discuss whatsoever. I'd appreciate it if you'll get out of my office."

Treva and Leona were walking down the hall together and overheard what Kutzie said.

Sternly, Leona reprimanded her. "Kutzie, I'm the boss around here and I alone have the authority to order someone to leave. What's going on anyway?"

Hey, Mrs. Lutz, old gal, I may buy this place if you don't straighten yourself up.

"I'll tell you what's going on." Bess butted in. "She and Rusty Hunt are sleeping together that's what's going on."

Leona narrowed her eyes, and glared at Bess. "Please leave this office. I'll speak to you shortly."

Turning to Kutzie, she asked, "Is that what you told her?"

Kutzie looked innocent. "Me tell her something like that? Of course not."

"Where did she get such an idea? Although granted, it's no one's business if you are or not," Leona replied. Treva stood there looking as if she were wondering which one told the lie.

"You know how she is." Kutzie answered. "I said nothing whatsoever to her about anything."

"Well, I guess I'm going to have to let her go. She used to be a good employee but she's not the same, and she's causing too many problems within the company."

"I think she's like jealous of Kutzie, myself." Treva replied, looking at Bess.

Kutzie said nothing else, and decided she wouldn't try to defend the trouble-making Bess for she had been out of line when she blurted out those words thus she deserved to lose her job.

Leona turned on her heel, and said as she walked out. "Remember what I said, Kutzie. If someone is annoying you, come to me rather than saying hateful words, all right? It's the best way I know to keep from having inner-office squabbles."

"All right, I will." Kutzie answered, wondering what Leona was referring to regarding 'hateful' words. Then she remembered that she hadn't yet mentioned to her boss that she was leaving. "By the way, Rusty is apparently on his way over here to pick me up so we can discuss business. Do you object to that?"

"What do you have to discuss anyway, so soon after you decided on next week's ads? Is it something entirely necessary?"

"Do you need me here for something?" Kutzie asked without answering her question, and Leona shrugged her shoulders.

"Well, I should be back in a little while. If anything should come up I'll call you." Kutzie said.

Rusty picked her up in a new Cadillac, which she fell in love with. She mentioned that was her favorite so far. "Then it's yours, my sweet, if you like it," he said sincerely.

"What? Are you kidding?"

"Of course I'm not kidding. You can either sell your Toyota

or give it to your little sister if she would like to have it, or whatever you want to do. We'll put this car in your name tomorrow."

She was delighted by his generosity and snuggled against him on the bench seat, which he said he had installed specifically, because the bucket seats were not comfortable to his back.

"Where are we going?" Kutzie inquired, glancing out the window wondering what vicinity they were driving through.

"To the airport. Mom and Dad were in Dallas at the house when I called there. They said they'd get the first flight out which happens to be arriving at 2:15 this afternoon. That's quick traveling for my mom because she used to take days to pack a bag. I guess she's learned to get ready faster since she's on the go as much as she is these days."

"You told them of our engagement?"

He nodded. "Yes and they're delighted. They can hardly wait to meet you."

"Oh, Rusty, I hope they like me. I'm scared."

"You needn't be. They're going to love you as I do, darling."

As he parked the car, and they hurried inside to the arrival gates Kutzie's palms were damp with sweat and her face clammy. She didn't know why she was nervous about meeting Rusty's parents, but she was even though she had psyched herself up not to be.

They walked through one of the gift shops in Hartsfield International, and Kutzie was not aware that it was the largest airport in the world but she was impressed with its size, as well as its beauty and layout. It was truly the place to "people-watch." She saw people of every race, creed, and color, dressed in every different garb imaginable. She could hardly keep up with Rusty, because she was gawking so and Rusty had a good laugh as he watched her and held her hand tightly. They sat down inside one of the coffee shops, ordered coffee, watching the clock so they could get to the gate on time where the Southwest Airlines plane would arrive from Dallas, Texas.

The time seemed to drag for Kutzie, for she was anxious to get the chore over and done with.

Finally the moment arrived. Their plane was landing, and people were deplaning and walking through the hallway. Rusty's neck was stretched like a crane, and finally, when he spotted Charles and Lana Hunt, he whooped with delight, and grasping Kutzie's hand ran toward the well-dressed couple. His parents caught sight of him just as he reached them, and they all hugged and kissed and patted shoulders, and all the things that loving families do when they haven't seen each other in awhile. Kutzie was not forgotten or ignored. Both of Rusty's parents seemed truly happy to meet her and hugged her warmly, telling her how very glad they were that she was to become their daughter-in-law. Charles mentioned that both their sons were about to settle down, and hopefully start a family before they became too old to enjoy grandbabies.

As they drove away from Hartsfield International, Rusty delicately turned the wheel of the El Dorado, as he rounded the corner of Riverdale Road, and headed toward Jimmy Carter Blvd. down Interstate-85, laughingly telling his parents that he had just given the Cadillac to Kutzie, because she admired it so much he wanted her to enjoy it. Lana gushed, "I think that's wonderful. What kind of car are you presently driving, Kutzie?"

"A Toyota Tercel," she answered. "When I bought my car last year I thought it was so cute. I still do, but I love this car. Rusty said I should give my younger sis the Toyota."

"Tell me about your family." Lana went on, smiling, seemingly genuinely interested in her soon-to-be daughter-in-law. Kutzie began telling her all about her immediate family but went on to tell her that her mother was a victim of Alzheimer's. Lana was devastated that Kutzie and her family had such a tragedy in their lives and when she said so, Kutzie implied that it was her mom suffering the tragedy more so than the family. Lana agreed but added that her mother was not as aware that she had a problem, as the family was, and they were going to be marked with such terrible memories during the coming months and would always have those memories for years to come.

Kutzie was grateful that her mother-in-law to-be was as understanding as she seemed to be about the debilitating, mind-destroying disease. It made her comfortable sharing her grief with another woman who understood what the family was going through.

As they pulled through the gates to the Hunt Estate, Charles sighed, "I still don't like driving into this jail-house. I can't stand to be fenced in like this. Guess I'm too old for this type of living."

Lana scoffed and squeezed his hand. When the four of them entered the house, all the household personnel seemed beside themselves with glee. Kutzie wondered if they all would eventually accept her as mistress of the house after she and Rusty were married, for it was obvious that they all loved Rusty's parents, especially Lana. The chefs had prepared a special meal for them, which obviously surprised Rusty since he had only casually mentioned to them that morning that he would be picking up his parents at the airport that day.

The celebration party lasted throughout the day, and Kutzie was stuffed from eating so much!

No one thought of the time until almost 6:00 P.M., when Kutzie suddenly remembered that Leona had expected her back at the office that day.

"Why in the world are you working, Kutzie?" Charles

wanted to know. "Why don't you quit your job and put your time and heart into planning the biggest blow-out of a wedding this town has never seen before?"

"I told her she could move in here with me." Rusty replied with pride, as he ogled Kutzie.

"Why don't you?" Lana asked, and Kutzie saw that she was serious. Astonished at their modern-day thinking, Kutzie knew there was no way her parents would ever think it would be all right if she moved in with her fiancé. It simply wasn't done in Charlotte, that she was aware of.

At Kutzie's insistence, Rusty took her to her apartment about 8:00 P.M. She pleaded too many chores to do and reluctantly he had taken her home promising to pick her up early the next morning to join them for breakfast. She remembered on the way that they had not brought the car, but he said he would bring it to her the next day. She was quite excited about it!

The next morning, Rusty called at 7:00 a.m. sharp. "Hi, darling, how's my beautiful doll this lovely morning? Can you make arrangements to go into your office late so you can join us for breakfast?"

"I'm sure I can, sweetheart, but Leona won't be in the office until 8:00 or so so I can't call yet. I suppose I can call her from somewhere else at that time. Where are we going to have breakfast?"

"Here at the house. I'm bringing your car to you, and Dad's driving one for us to come back home in. Be ready, sweetie. See you in about a half-hour, okay?"

"You're bringing the Cadillac? Oh Rusty, I can't wait!" She was overjoyed at the news!

"Thought we'd go ahead and bring it to you so it'll be available whenever you want to start driving it, but it'll be a couple of days perhaps before I get the time to get it changed into your name and to get the insurance in your name. Would you rather we drop it off at Elite, so you can drive it home?"

"I hardly know what to say, Rusty. No one has ever given me a car before. I'm completely awed, overwhelmed. I'm simply speechless. Thank you for your sweet generosity, darling." She had forgotten the question he asked.

"You're welcome, sweetheart. Well, why don't we drop it off at Elite, and then we'll come on over there after you." There was a hint of amusement in his voice because of her elation.

* * *

Lana was waiting for the three of them to get back to the mansion, because when they walked in, she said she was starving. She was sitting on the veranda drinking coffee, enjoying the cool breeze, dressed in a white billowing hostess gown. Kutzie thought she was beautiful.

One of the chief cooks prepared the special breakfast for the four of them, and they ate it while sitting on the veranda, laughing and talking, planning the largest wedding that would ever take place in the city of Atlanta. The date was set for June 15th, which was almost a year away.

Kutzie revealed to Rusty and his family that her lifelong dream was to be married in a lush garden, wearing a white lace dress with a train that was as long as a room. She laughed when she admitted it but Lana informed her that it was a normal dream for a young girl to have.

They accomplished quite a bit on the wedding plans, and when Kutzie said she should go to work before Leona fired her the other three thought it would be perfectly all right if that should happen.

Kutzie realized that they simply did not understand that she could not move in with Rusty if she lost her job as they seemed to think. Dallas, Texas must be a wild and wicked place to her way of thinking if that was normal for Texans, but it was not the way she was brought up.

* * *

Meanwhile, at the office that afternoon, Leona was beside herself wondering where Kutzie was and what she was doing? They already had the Hubbard account, so what else was there to do? Bill had not mentioned to anyone what Kutzie had told him about Rusty proposing marriage, so Leona did not know.

Watching the door like a hawk waiting for prey, she pounced on Kutzie immediately the next morning when she walked in. "Where in the world were you yesterday?" she wanted to know, eyes squinted. "Did you accomplish anything new that I should know about? You never bothered to call to let me know where you were or anything. Are you going to work for me or aren't you?"

"Well, Leona, Rusty asked me to marry him, and I said 'yes'. We've set the date for June of next year. I would say that's an accomplishment, wouldn't you?"

"Bosh!" was all Leona said, as she walked toward her office, and Kutzie knew that she didn't believe her.

"It's true," she retorted. "His parents are in town now, because he wanted them to meet me."

She turned to stare in Kutzie's face, searching it as if she could detect that she was lying to her. "Tell me the truth. I don't think Rusty Hunt will ever find the perfect girl. I don't believe ya."

Kutzie raised her right hand. "So help me." *You trust me to get the account but you don't trust me to get the man?*

"Do you mean to tell me that he really isn't gay?" Leona stretched her red lips into a wide smile. *So that was her reason for doubt!*

"No, Leona, believe me he isn't gay."

"Well, gollee. I guess all I can say is you're marrying into so much money. Congrats."

"Thanks, but Leona, while I appreciate the fact that he's wealthy I love him for himself. He's a sweet man and a gentleman."

"Oh, sure! Well, you hit the jackpot whatever the reason." Leona seemed to know her newest special employee very well. She walked toward her office, and Kutzie sat down at her own desk, working on other ads. Suddenly, she remembered she didn't know where Rusty had parked the Cadillac when they brought it over, and she promptly picked up the phone and called his office, hoping he had gone straight to work when he dropped her off.

He had. She could hardly wait until time to get off work so she could drive it. Rusty had given her one set of keys for it, and he had kept one set so he could lock it up when he left it there.

Bill walked by her office, and paused in front of her door. Then, dropping his eyes he just walked on by without any acknowledgment whatsoever and that crushed her. She wanted him to understand. But . . . understand WHAT? He understood that she was marrying Rusty Hunt. That was what was bothering him, and it was also bothering her.

* * *

As she drove home that afternoon, the beautiful Cadillac drove like a dream. She was assigned only the one parking space under the carport and when she moved her Toyota into an uncovered space and pulled her new car into the carport space, she stood there admiring it. She then walked over to her mailbox, and brought in her mail. She had a couple of letters from friends back home plus 'junk mail', and when she had read the letters she went out into the kitchen to get a glass of milk just as the phone rang. It was Bill. "Kutzie, I've been thinking about how I'm behaving like a spoiled child and I want to apologize. I want to remain your friend, regardless of whether you're married or single. Truce?"

"There's no reason for a 'truce', Bill," she sighed, relieved to hear him say those words. "There is no war here. I treasure your friendship and I only want you to feel comfortable around me."

"How could I be any way but comfortable around you? I'll always love you but as a friend okay? A BEST friend."

"Okay. I feel much better. Bill, I'm so glad you called. I've worried over this situation."

"Me, too. Wanta come over for sandwiches tonight? That's all I'm having." He was his old self once again, for which she was grateful.

"Why don't you come over here for hamburgers?" she asked. "I left some ground beef thawing in the fridge day before yesterday, so I have to cook it tonight, or throw it out because it'll ruin."

* * *

They were eating hamburgers when there was a knock on the door. "Who could that be?" Kutzie wondered aloud as she walked to the door and there stood Rusty smiling. "Sweetheart, you line has been busy for an hour or more. I was afraid it was going to get too late for me to come after you for dinner tonight. Mom and Dad have gone on over to Anthony's to wait for us. We made reservations there for 7:00, for the four of us."

She stood speechless for a moment, then echoed, "Anthony's?"

"Yes, it's a restaurant on Piedmont Road, not far from where I live in Buckhead. It's not over five minutes away from here. May I come in? I feel sort of silly standing out here on your porch."

She stepped aside, and he walked in. "Do I smell food cooking? Darling, you're not cooking dinner are you? I thought we had a standing date."

His assumption made her angry. How dare he begin their relationship by taking her for granted, assuming she was at his beck and call! Well, he was not going to do that; she didn't care who he was. She stiffened, and with an icy tone said curtly, "Yes, I did fix dinner tonight. And, I haven't been on the phone, Rusty, but I have two lines so I must've left the phone partially off the hook by mistake. I'm sorry you were getting a busy signal because we should've talked. Tell your parents that I'm sorry but I can't join you tonight. I'm very tired and I don't feel like going out again tonight."

He stood there with both hands in his pockets, a shocked expression across his face, as though he could not believe she had said those words. She reached over and opened the door. "I'll see you tomorrow then?" He stood motionless for a minute as if he could not comprehend that she was telling him to leave, but with a whipped-dog expression on his handsome face, he nodded and left, walking slowly at first then he practically ran to his car. She closed the door and walked back into the kitchen grateful for the wall between it and the living room because Rusty was not able to see that Bill was sitting at her dinette table.

"Rusty?" Bill asked, raising an eyebrow.

"Uh huh. I just made him very angry, and now we may be calling off our engagement even before we have time to announce it." She smiled, slightly upset with herself for being impatient with Rusty, especially since he had just given her a brand-new Cadillac! She could teach him not to take advantage of her nor take her for granted but perhaps she should start at a later date. She shouldn't rock the boat first thing. She had to get that red-headed temper under control!

She and Bill had a wonderful time together eating hamburgers, and drinking iced tea, and discussing the places Rusty had taken her to in the last couple of days. Plus, he gave her the new Cadillac just that day, she boasted. Bill seemed interested in what she and Rusty had been doing and smiled as she mentioned each new experience.

She felt bad for disappointing Rusty that evening when she remembered the generous gift of the car and told Bill so. He said he had overheard the conversation that had taken place between her and Rusty and he agreed that Rusty should have called to ask her rather than take it for granted that she would go out with him just because they were engaged. His encouragement helped a lot and she felt better about it.

Chapter Six

The Attack

She took a warm bath, donned her pajamas and went to bed with a magazine to read, to help her get sleepy. As she lay there reading, she heard a noise at the window and she froze with fright, and lay there unable to breathe because she was so frightened. She switched off the lamp beside her bed and slipped out from under the covers to go to the window to peek out to see if she could see where the noise was coming from. The exterior lights were not burning outside, as they usually were, and it was too dark to see anything. "Oh no. Not again," she said aloud as she crept into the living room to use the phone for she was too frightened to stay in the bedroom and use the one beside her bed. The noise was definitely coming from her bedroom window. A dim night-light was burning on the living room wall going into the dining area, and she dialed 911 in the semi-darkness, with heart pounding so, she held her chest. She told the person who answered that she thought a burglar was breaking in, and the emergency operator assured her someone would arrive shortly. She took her telephone book to the wall where the night-light was plugged in, and could barely make out Ricky's telephone number. She prayed he would be home and when he said "Hello," she breathed, "Ricky. Remember the guy I told you about that was always around? He's probably at my bedroom window right now trying to break in." She was on the verge of hysteria, trying desperately to control her emotions. Ricky seemed concerned when he heard the emotion in her voice, and with alarm in his own he asked, "Kutzie, did you ever buy yourself a gun?"

"No, Ricky. I intended to, but . . . Oh, my god, Ricky, the kitchen window pane just shattered on the floor. He's gone around to the kitchen and he's coming in! I can hear him coming in!" She dropped the phone before she heard him say he would be right over . . . and ran into the bedroom and closed the door, went to the closet and felt around in the dark for a high heeled shoe to hit with if he should open the door. She heard nothing more except her heart pounding inside her chest. Suddenly, there was a loud noise and then, angry voices. Someone called her name and she opened the closet door ever so slightly and peered out, surprised to see lights burning through out her apartment.

She entered the living room slowly and cautiously at first, with the high-heeled shoe still clutched in her hand, and her knuckles a bloodless white from gripping it so tightly. Policemen were all over the room, and one was holding Junior by one arm twisted behind him, as he snapped handcuffs on him. Those evil, cat-like eyes were glaring at her with the hatred she had seen in them the first time she lay eyes on the man.

"This man was inside the kitchen when we arrived." One of the men told her angrily. "We arrived just in time, it seems. Do you know who he is? We can't get a word out of him!"

"I know only that he's been stalking me," Kutzie answered, swallowing the fear that welled up in her throat. I don't know him. I do know he has no tongue so he can't talk." She didn't say how she knew that and no one asked. She didn't say that she knew his name and where he lived. That would take too long to explain.

The officer snapped the cuffs on Junior's wrist, and told Kutzie, while walking him through her front door, "We're taking this jerk in. However, we can't keep him locked up unless you come down in the morning to file charges against him."

Kutzie stood there shaking with chills, and she picked up the afghan from the back of the sofa and wrapped it around her shoulders. She answered through chattering teeth, "I will. Thank you very much!"

They all walked out, except one who told her kindly, "I'll see what I can do about closing up the kitchen window for you tonight. The night's much too chilly to leave it open like it is, and it's an open invitation to other burglars. That man isn't the only one out there breaking in, you know. However, we seldom have any problems in this area."

Kutzie nodded, still shivering. The officer walked out into the kitchen, saying, "You sit there and get yourself calmed down, and I'll see what I have in my car that I can use to fix your window for the time being."

Kutzie nodded, wondering what the neighbors must think.

When the patrolman walked back inside, Ricky was with him. He rushed to Kutzie's side, and she fell against him, throwing both arms around his neck, sobbing hysterically. "There, there," he said, stroking her face and kissing her forehead, as though she were a child. He picked her up in his arms, walked over and sat down on the sofa holding her on his lap. After awhile, she began to calm down and Ricky looked up to see that the other officer was back, and standing there waiting to talk with him.

"Yes?" Ricky asked.

"Do you know the man we picked up? Are you familiar with the circumstances at all?"

Ricky gently set Kutzie on the sofa and he stood up and shoved both hands into his pockets.

"Yes, I'm familiar with the case enough to know that this young lady recently moved to Atlanta and this person, Junior somebody, immediately started showing up around the apartments for no apparent reason, and then over at Miss Kline's job site as well. The guy's a schitzo more than likely and needs to be locked up before he hurts somebody."

"Well, Sergeant Akers explained to Miss Kline she would have to come to the station to file charges, or we can't hold him."

"I'll see that she does that. Thanks." Ricky said and the two men shook hands and Ricky showed him to the door. Then he walked back and scooped Kutzie up and set her on his lap once again.

She had not even realized that she had no robe on over her satin pajamas, but Ricky must have. He stroked her soft body pulling her against his own hard muscles, and rubbed his hands over her shoulders and down her back gently at first then the strokes became more intense, as he ran his hands down her sides and back to her shoulders once again. When his hands glided to her buttocks Kutzie relaxed against him, purring like a kitten. Neither realized it was going to happen. It just did.

Afterwards, they were lying on the bed, facing each other with total shock on their faces. Finally, Ricky smiled shrugging his shoulders, "I can't say I'm sorry this happened. It's what I've dreamed of since the moment I met you."

She buried her head into his shoulder cupping her palms around her face. "I'm so ashamed, Ricky. How could I be so weak? I'm engaged to be married. How could this happen?"

"Engaged? Who in the world to? Surely, not to that fellow you work with that you went out with last Saturday night?" He looked stricken. *And what would be wrong with that if I were?* Aloud, she said, "No, not to him. To Rusty Hunt."

"The big shot of Atlanta? Mister Rich Guy? No way! Since when have you two been so well-acquainted? I know about that guy. The papers say he's a confirmed bachelor."

"He was the 'JOB' I had when I first moved here," she snapped. "Elite needed Hubbard's business, and I was hired to convince him we could do a better job than the advertising company they had been using. We fell in love. Now, he will no longer be a confirmed bachelor!"

"So, you not only got the company the business, you also got the boss of the store for yourself?"

He sounded angry, so she asked, "Are you angry?"

"Your damn right I am. I thought you were about the sweetest breath of air to pass through this city, and I hoped to get to know you better. I'm very disappointed that right off the bat you're going to marry some jack-ass you hardly know."

"What do you mean, 'jack-ass'? Because he's marrying me? Well, I'll have you know, Ricky Larson, it was a situation where Rusty and I just hit it off. I still would like to remain friends with you if you'll stop being such a spoil-sport. I fell for Rusty because I feel he will be very good for me."

"Oh, bullshit. I would be good for you, too. Do you expect me to be happy over this announcement? You belong to me!" he snapped. "See how compatible we would be? We just melted together a little while ago without either of us knowing it was going to happen."

She turned over, and stood up reaching for her robe. "I think you should leave, Ricky." she whispered as she stepped into the pants and then pulled the shirt on. "But, thank you so much for coming over to see about me."

"Any time, Kutzie. And, yes we can remain friends. I want to tell you that I hope you'll be happy with the old coot."

"He's not old, Ricky. He's probably younger than you are. He's only thirty."

"Well, I've never seen him that I know of, and don't care if I never do." He stepped into his shoes, and stood up to button his shirt, and then stuffed the shirt-tail into his trousers. He stood there looking at her for a full minute, then grabbed her and kissed her hard on the lips, not only taking her breath away with the suddenness of it, but it hurt her. Then he slapped her on the rear, and saluted a 'good-bye' in the same way as when she saw him that first time.

She sat there on the side of the bed thinking on the events of that evening. It all seemed so devastating it was hard to comprehend what had truly occurred. Yet, rather than being totally a terrible thing that had happened between her and Ricky, it had been a beautiful event. Devastating, nevertheless, simply because she belonged to another man now. She finally went back to bed and after a long period of time, fell asleep. The ringing of the telephone woke her. She hadn't set her alarm the night before, and surely, she had overslept. Had it not been for Rusty calling, she would have. His voice was calm, and a tad cool when she answered. "Good morning," and he asked soberly, "Do you feel better this morning?"

She detected the coolness at once. "Yes, I think I do. How are you, Rusty?"

"Not too good, I'm afraid. I had a miserable time last night and could hardly wait until morning arrived, so I could call you and apologize."

And, she had intended to be the one to apologize. "Apologize? For what?" She asked complacently.

"For assuming you would have dinner with us last night. I thought we had discussed it when we were all together yesterday, but evidently we didn't. I'm sorry."

"I would've gone, Rusty but I fixed a bite to eat here, and it was best that I stayed in anyway."

She longed to tell him about Junior, and what had taken place the night before, but she didn't want to have to start from the beginning, and she didn't have the time. She had never told him about the man and certainly was not ready to bring it up at the moment.

"My mom says she'd like to spend some time with you tonight. Are you free?" His tone was so formal!

"Of course I'm free, you silly you!" she thought she would tease him a little. It seemed to work.

His voice became jovial. "Good. Then, I'll either send Brian to pick you up, or one of us will, when you get off work."

"And, then you'll bring me back here for my car? Oh, Rusty, I love that car!"

"Good, I'm glad. Well, why don't I send Brian over to your apartment to pick you up this morning, and take you to work? Then, he can pick you up this afternoon, and you won't have to worry about driving at all today."

"Hey, guy, did you hear me? I love that car. You're not doing me any favors by having someone pick me up so I won't have to drive. But hey, that's fine. I'll be ready to leave here around 8:15."

But she needed to go to the police station and file charges against Junior. When would she be free to do that if she wasn't going to have a car today? Perhaps she would take a cab . . .

Hurriedly she dressed, thinking of Bill the entire time. But, then she always did. He was the first thing she thought of each morning and the last thing she thought of at night. She could hardly wait to see him each morning at work. But, she was going to have to forget him. She only thought of him because he was the first friend she made when she moved to Atlanta, she thought to herself. He meant nothing to her as far as romantic feelings went. He would simply remain one of her best friends. *Oh, yeah, only a friend? Then, why do you always wonder what it would be like to make love with him?*

Brian was waiting for her when she walked outside at promptly 8:15.

She strutted into Elite with her white pleated skirt swinging around the curvature of her hips with each step she took in her red 3-inch heels. Her sweater was blood red, and loose, yet it caressed her bosom softly. She wore a white scarf around her neck, and carried a blood red purse.

Treva was standing near the door when Kutzie walked in, and smiling, she replied, "I don't see how in the world you like work in high heels. I have to like wear flats, or I'd be falling on my face like at the end of the day."

"If I had to do a lot of standing I'd wear flats, also." Kutzie admitted. "But, I don't have any problems with high heels really."

Bess walked up with papers in her hand and she stuck her chin up when she saw Kutzie, and leered. "So, you're not going to Hubbard's these days? What happened anyway, he won't see you anymore?"

Kutzie rolled her eyes, and swept past her without a word. Leona, observing it all from across the room, said, "Okay, Bess, that's one. Remember you have only three more chances." Kutzie wondered why she didn't just fire Bess' butt right then!

Kutzie hurried toward Bill's office, but he was not there. Why, she wondered? Where would he be? She hurried into the file room, but he was not there. She went into the supply room, but he was nowhere to be found. When she finally spotted him at the front door, she walked up behind him and walked her fingers up his spine, asking what he was doing relieved he was there on the job. He turned and looked down at her, "Watching the clouds. We're under a tornado warning."

"I didn't know! I haven't had my radio on this morning. Mmmm, those clouds do look ominous, don't they?" She stood on tiptoe, straining to see over one of his shoulders pressing against him as she did so, although the act was not necessary for she had plenty of room to stand beside him and see outside. As he turned, he looked at her with a sober look and wiped a hand across his forehead. At that moment the thunder rolled with a loud boom, and the lightning flashed wildly, streaking to the ground, and the clouds became blacker, and churned fiercely. She put both arms around him, and then he turned completely around, and held her in his arms, grasping her tightly.

For blessed moments, neither of them moved. They simply stood there holding on to each other without saying a word for no words needed to be said. When they heard Leona's footsteps patting down the carpeted hall, Kutzie moved back, and looked up at him with saddened eyes. He turned on his heel and walked toward the doorway that Leona was walking through at the same time. "Kutzie, are you going to go out in this weather? The weather man is saying to stay inside, and to go to a place of shelter immediately." She had a frightened expression, Kutzie then noticed for the first time.

"I was, but I don't think I want to go out. I'll call Rusty to tell him. Oh, shoot! I don't have my car today. Brian, one of Rusty's limo drivers, picked me up today, so I wouldn't have to drive. I didn't know stormy weather had been predicted."

"Wouldn't you like rather have someone drive you to work, and back home again, when the weather's like this, rather than your having to drive in it yourself?" Treva asked, walking through the door at the time. Kutzie wondered why they were all gathering in the front lobby like this, when no one hardly ever went in there. "I guess so. I'd really rather not have to be out in this at all, regardless of who's driving," she answered rationally.

Kutzie forgot about going to the police station, almost as soon as she remembered she needed to go but had no car. Once, she considered asking Bill that if he were going out for lunch, would he mind dropping her by the station, but changed her mind when she remembered how the traffic becomes so heavy in the downtown area at noontime, she didn't want to ask that of him. She wondered about calling a cab, but had heard how the drivers drove so fast, it was scary. So the thought slipped her mind, and when Rusty called to ask if she was ready for Brian to come for her to bring her to his place she said she was. It was almost 4:30 and the rain had stopped, although the skies were yet cloudy when Brian arrived, and Rusty was with him, and when he opened the back door for her she was surprised to see him sitting there grinning. He pulled her into his arms and kissed her fully on the lips. "I had to see you. I couldn't wait another minute." he told her, kissing her cheeks, her forehead, and then, her lips once again. She held him tightly around the neck, loving his arms around her, feeling warm and fuzzy within them.

"I'm sorry about last night," she whispered, but he would never know what she was sorry for.

When they arrived at the gates to the mansion, Kutzie straightened up and took her compact from her handbag that he had bought her when they went shopping and powdered her nose and applied fresh lipstick. Rusty smiled and said she was beautiful enough.

Charles and Lana were waiting in the study. Charles was puffing on a long cigar, stretched out in a big leather recliner, and Lana was thumbing through travel brochures. When they came into the room Lana stood up, and walked over to Kutzie and hugged her, which made Kutzie feel kind of special and also surprised her. Charles too, hugged her, mentioning their disappointment the night before when she was unable to join them for dinner. He added that the meal was delectable. She apologized for not being able to join them at the restaurant but Lana assured them they would make up for it during the next several days for she had made plans for them all. The next few days were filled.

Practically every day the Hunt's picked Kutzie up, either in the Lincoln or the Rolls limo. She was becoming quite spoiled. Usually she was taken to the store and sometimes to the house to pick up Rusty and then they usually joined Lana and Charles. Their favorite meeting place was at the Country Club were Charles usually played golf.

Kutzie was having a hard time finding excuses to get away from work because Leona was no longer interested in her seeing Rusty Hunt very often, since it looked as though the Hubbard account was theirs for a long time, yet she was probably afraid not to allow her the time off she requested, at least part of the time, lest she convince Rusty to cancel the contract they were drawing up.

* * *

Lana and Kutzie went to a Bridal Salon in the mall one evening, and Kutzie selected her wedding dress. The next day, she and Rusty chose their rings, and later at his home he slipped the engagement ring on her third finger, left hand, in the presence of his parents who applauded when he kissed her. Afterwards, they celebrated with champagne.

In all the hoopla Kutzie never intended to neglect her family, but other than when she called to tell them of her engagement to Rusty, she had not called them since. When she returned home each evening there was always a message on the machine from either Richard or Amber. But it was always too late to call. She did not want to wake them and she knew she would if she called when she came in. It seemed to her that Lana and Charles were always in a hurry as if they were anxious to get somewhere else. When they were out together Kutzie always felt that they would be taking her to her apartment shortly without a fuss, for surely there must be something to do somewhere else without her presence.

Lana was bubbly, yet sophisticated to the highest degree.

One Saturday during breakfast she announced that she and Charles were flying to Greece the next day and probably would not be back until Christmas when they would proceed with the wedding plans. She thought that would be the perfect time to mail out the wedding invitations.

Kutzie already loved them both dearly and knew she would miss them, but nothing she or Rusty could say persuaded them to change their minds and stay.

After the meal was over Kutzie asked if they would drop her off at her place as she had telephone calls to make and letters to write. She simply HAD to call her folks. When Rusty asked why she didn't make the calls from his home she explained that she also had other things to do. He asked if she would go with him to take his parents to the airport the next day and she said she would.

Because Kutzie spent almost every non-working hour with Rusty and his parents and even a portion of her work days many times, she could not remember when she had called her parents last. She knew they were always in bed by 10:00 p.m. and she refused to wake them. So, days turned to weeks and finally months, because she kept telling herself she did not want to wake them. Once or twice, because Lana insisted, Kutzie spent a night at the mansion and occasionally on those nights she thought of calling but each time she would change her mind thinking she would call from her own apartment, and another night passed by and she didn't.

During those weeks, she did not see Junior and seldom gave him a thought anymore. She had forgotten that she had never gone to the police station to file charges but he would have already been released before then anyway.

Kutzie, Lana, Charles and Rusty planned to have dinner together that night so they could say their goodbyes to each other, and afterwards Rusty would take her home. As they approached the front door, she immediately spotted the huge footsteps in the dirt at her bedroom window, but said nothing. The sprinkler system automatically went on each day at dusk, and she knew that the footprints were from the night before.

Junior again!

My god, she had momentarily forgotten about him!

Rusty unlocked the front door, handed her the key and as he kissed her good-bye he whispered he loved her and left.

She ran inside and dialed Ricky's phone number.

"Ricky, it's Kutzie. Remember when you suggested I buy a gun? Will you please go with me tonight to show me what kind I should buy?"

"You've finally decided to, huh?" he asked, "Great! The sooner the better! Has he been back?"

"Yes, last night. I've put up with this as long as I intend to. I may have to shoot the gun in the air to scare him to let him know I mean business, but I do mean business now."

"I'll pick you up in twenty minutes," he told her. "The gun shop will close in 30 minutes. We'll have to hurry."

When they walked into the gun shop, she felt strange and out of place. She had never in her wildest dreams imagined herself buying a gun. But, never would she have dreamed that she would be stalked by a stranger she had never seen before she moved to Atlanta who did not know her and had no reason to stalk her, other than out of sheer meanness.

She purchased a thirty-two semi-automatic, because Ricky assured her it was easy to use and not too expensive. When they arrived back at her apartment he walked around her place checking out the footprints, and when he went inside, announced that the prints were at every window. "Evidently, he tried every one of the windows, and when he couldn't pry them open he must have left. Looks like when the maintenance crew replaced that window for you in the kitchen, after the last time Junior visited you, they did a very good job in making them secure. Why didn't you call me when you heard him last night?"

She ignored the question. "Ricky, I never did go to the police station and file charges against that man. Things kept cropping up and I just never got around to doing it."

"Well, it doesn't matter now but if he bothers you again you need to, so they can hold him in jail. That's the only way they can. Please be careful, Kutzie. And, if you ever get him inside your door and you pull the gun on him don't try to just scare him with it. If you aim it shoot! Don't hesitate a second. Remember, you're to protect yourself. And kill the bastard but wait until he gets inside your home."

His words were frightening. "It's loaded now?" she asked, not knowing if she wanted him to say it was or wasn't.

"It's loaded with six bullets each more powerful than the other. If you have to shoot six times the sixth bullet will tear him apart. Those are police bullets, sweetheart, and they'll stop him, I guarantee that! When you shoot, remember squeeze the trigger. Don't pull it."

She thanked him, and when he left she finally dialed her folks in Charlotte. Their answering machine came on, and the message said only that they were unable to answer the phone right now. Kutzie left a message explaining that because she had been so busy with her wedding plans that was her first chance to call at a decent hour.

Next, she gathered together her laundry and went outside to the Laundromat and put it in a washer making sure she locked her front door as she left. When the clothes were washed she hurried back inside, hoping she had not missed the return call from her folks. She hadn't.

She had the clothes put away, and was watching television when Amber called. "Kootie? Gollee, we haven't heard from you in so long, we were really worried about you. Your message said you were so busy with the wedding plans you haven't had a chance to call? I would have loved to help you with those plans."

Guilt swept over Kutzie, for she had never even given her little sister a thought in helping her.

"I'm sorry, Amber but I'd thought you might want to help on deciding the colors for my wedding? I thought about lilac and peach. What do you think?" She had not even thought of any colors before that very minute, but she didn't want her sister to know she had neglected her . . .

"I think those would be beautiful together. I would like to go with you to choose your wedding dress. That would be a lot of fun!"

"Honey, Rusty's mother has already picked it out. After all, she's footing the bill so I didn't say anything. But, will you be my maid of honor?"

"Oh, Kootie, yes I'd be honored to." It seemed Amber was so delighted at hearing her sister's voice she would have agreed to anything Kutzie said. As they giggled, and chatted, nothing was said about anything being wrong, or being out of the ordinary, but, when Richard took the phone he told his older daughter with great sadness in his voice, that they had to place Melissa into a nursing home the week before. Kutzie saw red immediately wondering why Amber had so conveniently forgotten to mention that fact. She tried to control the rush of emotions that ran through her, suddenly overpowering her and causing her to feel like running and screaming through the streets. She wanted to scream at her father but of course, she would never do that no matter what he may have done. So, she gathered herself together and in a rational, composed tone of voice simply said, "You did? Was she that bad so suddenly?"

"Sweetheart, it hasn't been at all sudden. She's been bad for awhile, but I think we closed our eyes to it for far too long. There were lots of things that took place that I never told you girls about, and there were times that I was afraid she was going to harm herself, or one of us."

"Dad! Really? Why? What was going on?" She amazed herself that she managed to speak as calmly as she did.

"Well," he drawled, "She needs medical attention we were no longer able to give her, for one thing, Honey. But, she . . . uh . . . she . . . uh . . . tried to choke Amber, and tried to stab me with a paring knife. She no longer knows right from wrong, and doesn't realize what she's doing and didn't mean to harm us but of course, it could have been a dangerous situation if we had not been paying attention. So . . .", then his voice broke, "Amber and I decided that was where she needed to be. We've tried to reach you several times to see what you'd have to say about it but when we were unable to we made the decision. You understand don't you, that we would never have done such a thing if we did not feel that it was best for your mother. You know how much we love her."

She calmed down somewhat, as he spoke realizing that what he said made sense. Richard loved his wife very much and everyone recognized that so if that was his decision then it was right. She said nothing at first, then mumbled, "Okay, Dad. I understand. I really do understand. It's all right. I think I'll drive over there tomorrow and spend the day. I think I had already told Amber I wanted to."

"Do that, Dear. We would love to see you."

Next, she called Rusty explaining that she needed to go to

Charlotte and would he please tell his parents how happy she was to have met them, and ask them to keep in touch while they were gone, explaining she had to get some things ready in order to go to her parents' home.

He promised he would, and that he hoped things weren't too bad in Charlotte, and to please call him when she returned.

She left at 6:30 A.M. the next morning, hoping to arrive about the time they would be rising.

Her father greeted her at the door hugging her fondly, showing how very glad he was to see her. He put on the coffee, while Kutzie ran giddily upstairs to wake Amber. She wasn't there! Puzzled, she ran back downstairs, asking where Amber had gone to so early in the morning?

Richard took a deep breath, and sighed, "She's moved in with her boyfriend, Randy. She said she couldn't bear to see your mother in the condition she's in." He gestured with spread hands. "So, she left." He dropped his tired eyes as he spoke. Kutzie didn't know whether to be angry with her sister but she did not understand how she could move away like that. And, why hadn't she told her THAT when they talked the night before? Melissa was in a nursing home so Amber's reason for leaving home did not make sense. Kutzie thought it was because Amber did not want any responsibility.

Suddenly, the thought came to mind that she herself had done the same thing when she moved to Atlanta, and she instantly felt ashamed. For a moment she stood looking at her father wearing a sad expression on his face and, somberly she walked into the kitchen to pour them a cup of coffee. When she returned, and sat beside him, she said, "I'd like to go out to see Mom. Wouldn't you?"

He nodded. "Yes, I would. I'd planned to go out there just as soon as I ate a bite of breakfast."

"Let's go to The Cracker Barrel, and eat breakfast, then go on from there." She suggested. "It'll take less time, because we won't have to clean up dishes."

They went to the restaurant and had a quick bite then to the nursing home. Melissa was asleep when they arrived and when Kutzie kissed her forehead, she opened her eyes and stared angrily at her. "Who are you?" she mumbled, incoherently.

Kutzie smiled. "You know who I am, Mom. I'm your daughter, Kutzie."

"I never saw you before in my life," Melissa said a little more coherent and louder and outwardly agitated. Kutzie straightened up, confused and hurt because her own mother didn't know who she was. She stood there a moment then suddenly turned and ran from the room stifling the sobs she could not control. She broke down in the lobby crying out all the pent-up emotions she had kept under wraps for weeks. The nursing aids attempted to console her but when Richard walked out to see about her she told him she wanted to leave! Sadly, he said, "Honey, your mother cannot help it because her memory is gone and she doesn't recognize any of us. We love her anyway and she needs to know that. This is a disease no one can control. She needs all our love and understanding. Please go back in there and say something to her that may help her remember who you are. Please?"

She looked up at him, wiping her nose with a tissue and wiped the tears spilling down her face. Then, as she stood up she said, "I will, Dad. I'm ashamed of myself."

She went back into her mother's room and tried to carry on a conversation with her speaking of past occasions such as seasons of celebrations, their birthday parties when she and Amber were children, but nothing made the frown leave Melissa's face and she never said another word to Kutzie. They stayed an hour or more with her, and when they left Kutzie was absolutely spent! They drove back to the house and she went directly into Amber's room to lie down. She didn't realize how tired she was, but it was after 2:00 p.m. when Amber touched her shoulder, waking her. She sat up and they hugged each other. Then Kutzie blurted out all that had happened at the nursing home, and that Mom was so pitiful she could hardly stand it. Amber reminded her she had told her so. She explained that the reason she had to move out of the house, was because living there was the same as living alone. Dad was at the nursing home most of the time, and when he was home, he was depressed, and was depressing. She thought he would fare better if she were not there for him to worry about. Kutzie asked if she thought he didn't worry about her living with her boyfriend? Amber did not answer that. She simply said that they were getting married in December. Kutzie asked questions about the new boyfriend, and Amber told her he was an intern, studying now to become an ob-gyn instead of a veterinarian as was originally planned. They had fallen hard for each other—FAST. Kutzie offered her regards and then informed her of the latest on hers and Rusty's upcoming marriage in June of next year, suggesting that she and Randy postpone their marriage and they would have a double wedding. Amber said only that it was a nice thought but she'd have to see what Randy thought about it. Each expressed hope that their Mom would be able to attend their weddings by that time. Amber said sadly. "Dad's grieving so, he's going to be down sick himself if Mom doesn't improve. I hope HE'S able to attend our weddings as well, but he seems to be going downhill all the time, and I've worried about him." Kutzie didn't necessarily agree.

Driving back to Atlanta that evening, Kutzie almost wished she had not seen her mother in the condition she was in, yet she couldn't hide from the truth.

Upon arriving home, the first thing she thought of was the pistol she had bought the day before and, for some unexplainable reason, she walked straight to her bedroom, and removed it from the bag it came in and put it into her handbag. She may keep it in her car in case she ever broke down again on the streets somewhere, she thought. Then, she called Rusty, who was waiting impatiently to hear from her, which she knew he would be. He asked if he could come over but she said she was tired and depressed and wanted only to go to bed. He said he loved her, they said their goodnights and hung up. She wanted to talk to Bill and once or twice, started to look up his number where she had written it in her book, but she never did. Instead, she went to bed, and dreamed about him.

The next day at work, she wore a forced smile telling no one about her sad weekend. Bess asked if she were going to stay in the office all day or did she plan to hurry over to Hubbard's?

Kutzie looked at her without answering at first, then said simply, "I haven't decided."

Treva smiled at Kutzie, chewing gum with all the power she had in her jaws, and said, "You look like you're tired, Kutzie." Kutzie nodded but assured her she was fine.

Leona walked in complaining about the traffic. "It's hell fighting that congested morning traffic all the way from George Busbee Parkway." she fumed.

"Why don't you move closer in?" Bill asked, just walking in the door. Leona looked at him as though he had insulted her and growled, "That would be even worse as far as I'm concerned."

Kutzie went to her office to see which projects she should start on before she left to go to Hubbard's, for she was sure Rusty would be calling. She found it hard to concentrate because her thoughts were on her parents and what she should do about staying where she was or if she should move back to Charlotte, and get a job so she could be near them and take care of them.

When the telephone rang, it startled her so that she jumped. It was Rusty, asking if she would have lunch with him. She said she would unaware that Bill had been standing outside her door observing her with a worried expression on his face. When she hung up, he walked in and sat down just looking at her. Finally, he asked, gently, "What's wrong, Sweetheart?" That was all he said, and she started to cry. He jumped up, and rushed to her side and held her tightly. "What is it?" She dropped her head onto his chest, and wiped her eyes with a tissue. "It's my mother. She's so pitiful. She doesn't even know me anymore!" And, she cried louder. He stood holding her, patting her, rubbing her shoulder, as he consoled her until finally, she raised her head, and smiled at him. "Thank you, darling."

Loosening his grip, he looked at her, and his eyes widened with surprise. He said softly, "Please don't call me that unless you mean it, okay?"

"I do mean it. With all my heart. I only wish . . ."

"What?" he knitted his brow. "What do you wish, Kutzie?"

"I only wish that . . . oh, uh . . . nothing. It wasn't important."

"Kutzie, If I stand a chance with you please tell me. I'm going crazy! I can't stand the thought of your marrying that Hunt guy. You're mine, not his! I love you too much to let you go unless you tell me you want me to leave you alone."

"Well, I love both of you and I don't know what to do."

"Kutzie, you don't love both of us. You can't mean that."

She looked at the carpet on the floor. "I do mean it, Bill . . . I . . . wish . . ."

She blinked, taking a tissue from the box on her desk, knowing she wasn't making a whole lot of sense but also was unable to explain exactly how she felt.

"Why are you marrying that man? I know you aren't marrying him for his money, but I know you can't possibly love him either because you love me! You can't love both of us."

"I do love both of you." she sniffed softly, holding the tissue to her nose.

"Why, you won't even look me in the eye when you say that, Sweetheart. Well, I'll be waiting no matter how long it takes for you to find out he's not the one you want. I haven't proposed to you because I wanted you to be sure of your feelings before I mentioned the word 'marriage'. I knew I loved you when I saw the photo you mailed to Leona last April. I always will. I'll wait for you forever if I have to."

She interrupted him, and wanting to shut out the words he was saying to her, she snapped, "I do know him, and I do love him, and I will marry him, and I don't wish to continue this discussion."

She turned her head before he saw her eyes brimming with tears again. She was concerned that she so easily became emotional lately. He looked at her with the saddest eyes she had ever seen and walked out of her office. She wondered for a fleeting instant if money was worth having to give him up. Trying to concentrate on her work that day took every fiber of her being for her thoughts kept drifting back to Bill and what he had said. She thought again of her family and wondered for the thousandth time if she should go back to Charlotte to care for her father. He seemed to need her more than her mother did. She worried that he may not be eating properly, and knew that her mother was. She had noticed when she was home the last time, that the fridge was well-stocked with food, and there was even left-overs from a previous meal, so someone was cooking.

When Rusty walked in at 12:05, she was extremely happy to see him. As they walked to his car arm in arm, she was smiling.

His timely arrival made her realize he was the man in her life, not Bill Davis.

She told Rusty how her mother behaved when she went to visit her at the nursing home, and what a strain her illness had put on everyone. She even told him that Amber had moved in with her boyfriend. He sympathized and attempted to console her. He asked if Amber wanted the Tercel, and she told him she didn't. He said he would place an ad in the daily paper advertising it for sale as he had told her he would from the start, for which she was thankful; she had no idea whatsoever how much the car was worth, although it was in excellent condition.

They planned to eat lunch at the Swan Coach House Restaurant because it was not too far from Rusty's home and he wanted to stop by his house and make some phone calls first. He planned to call the daily paper and place an ad to sell her Toyota along with other calls he wished to make as well.

While he was on the phone, she wandered through the house considering what it was going to be like living in a mansion. She planned where to place certain pieces of her furniture, such as the old recliner that was once her father's. She may even have it re-upholstered, she thought, depending on her mood when the time came. She could hardly wait until she was moved in! She loved the house, and already felt at home.

She heard Rusty calling her name as he walked through the house, and she smiled to herself as she thought how easy it would be to hide from someone in a house that size. He could search for her for days, and never find her. No one would know where a person was unless that person wanted to be found. They ran into each other in the foyer.

"Well, my telephone calling's done," he told her as they walked out to his car. "I made a few business calls while I was here, besides calling the newspaper. Sometimes, it's hard to make certain calls from the office, when there's always interruptions. Besides, it's hard to remember all I want to say to certain people when I'm calling from my office. Make sense?"

"I thought Donna Sue made all your telephone calls for you?" she commented.

"Well, most, but not all. Some calls are personal, such as these today. I talk to my attorney once in awhile about things, plus I sometimes talk to old friends in Dallas."

He pulled out of the circle drive, and drove to the restaurant, where they enjoyed a scrumptious meal and each other's company. Kutzie relished the attention the wait-people lavished on them, noticing that Rusty was a generous tipper which could account for the fact that people bent over backwards to please him. They had an enjoyable time and when it was time to return to Elite he asked her if she could go over to the store for awhile. She said she was sorry, but she was involved with other work which needed to be finished. She wondered what he had in mind when he asked that. On the drive over to Elite he then asked if she would come to his home for supper that night.

"I plan to grill steaks, and we'll have the entire house to ourselves except for Rodney the butler, and he's been told not to answer the phone, nor the door."

"The door? No one ever comes to your front door. They can't get through the gates, can they?" She assumed he was attempting to make a point.

He took both her hands in his right one and squeezed them gently, as he winked an eye teasingly. Immediately, Kutzie was suspicious of his motives else why would he give all his household personnel the night off? *Does he think I'll give in to him again as I did the other morning? Oh, no, he wouldn't manipulate me.* She had told him she never would again, until after they were married and she was not going to.

She simply smiled and said she would love to join him for dinner at his home. She could handle him all right. He walked her back inside the building saying he would pick her up at her apartment as soon as she arrived there. Again, Kutzie detected the jealousy exuding from her peers, especially Bess, as they entered. Treva stood smiling and the old man, Louis Shaw, simply shook his head, sauntering off to the supply room. Leona was staring into the computer screen. Bill was out of the office selling advertising, and Kutzie missed him so much all afternoon. She thought 4:30 would never arrive. It was the first time since coming to Elite that she was actually anxious for the day to end. Not because she was anxious to see Rusty again that night . . . at least, she didn't think so. It was because Bill always came back into the office by quitting time. What was wrong with her? What did she want, anyway? When would Bill return to the office? Where was he, that he had been gone most of the afternoon? He had a customer that he had to call on earlier in the day but . . .

After work she drove home slowly, and found Rusty waiting. When she parked, he stepped out of the Mercedes and opened her door to help her out. She felt somewhat better at that moment than she had when she left the office. He smiled at her, and led her to her door with her arm in his. "Mother said to tell you she left clothes in a closet for you to wear while you're visiting me. Sometimes it isn't convenient to pack a bag first."

She unlocked the door herself, saying lightly, "Cool. I doubt that I'll be changing clothes there, but I guess it's nice to know that."

* * *

Driving into Buckhead was as always, an experience, it was

so breathtakingly beautiful as well as relaxing. When the gates swung open for Rusty to drive onto the grounds, Kutzie sighed, feeling that she was home again. Funny, how the mansion had suddenly become so much more like home to her than her own little apartment lately. Perhaps because she had adjusted to the understanding that it was going to be her home in only a year, and especially, since she had stayed over several times. Besides, she had already arranged her furniture in it in her mind.

Rusty parked on the circular drive, and the double doors swung open as if by magic, for them to enter. The butler bowed, and greeted them cheerfully. Rusty took Kutzie's arm and led her out to the veranda. "Isn't this the perfect spot to have dinner tonight?" he asked.

She glanced around and nodded. "It is beautiful, Rusty. The trees are so full of leaves and the foliage has thickened almost to the point of being a forest." He laughed in agreement.

"Which of your servants did you say you had given the evening off?" Kutzie inquired although she remembered what he had originally told her; she was only making conversation.

"All but Rodney the butler," he answered. "And he's been told not to disturb us under any circumstances."

"You're not expecting company tonight? Seems like I remember your mom saying they'd be back in town today. Will they call first, or come on out?"

She wondered how far he had gone to plan this night out.

"Well, my brother Chris has a remote, and of course, Mother and Dad does, but we know they won't be driving up, remember? I don't actually expect anyone. Chris would have called if he were going to be in town and since he hasn't I don't expect anyone. Otherwise, this dinner would've been planned for a different night."

And, as he said it he was wrapping his arms around her, and he began kissing her ardently.

When she realized that he had expected to make a night of it after all, she was infuriated. He obviously had not believed her when she told him she did not intend to sleep with him again until after they were married. He had even told her after they made love that first time that he was sorry, and had not meant for it to happen, and tonight he had planned to seduce her. Were all men alike, as her Aunt Susie used to say so often, years ago?

"What are we having for dinner anyway?" Kutzie said, not meaning to sound so harsh, as she turned her face away so he could not kiss her.

"Tasha said she'd leave our dinner in the oven. She named off all kinds of wonderful dishes she had prepared for us." His voice was calm and even yet he seemed agitated.

Kutzie strolled into the kitchen and opened the oven door. Tasha was right! All kinds of beautiful, good-smelling food was waiting for them. Even the table had been set ahead of time. All they had to do was to carry the food from the oven to the veranda, and Kutzie loaded her arms trying to balance the warm dishes so she would not burn herself. All the time she was wishing she had brought her own car. She may have to leave ardent Rusty by himself before the evening got started.

Rusty seemed surprised when he saw her carrying the food from the oven to the table.

"Are we going to eat right now?" he asked, as he switched off the lights except for one dim one that barely glowed that was hanging above the veranda table.

"I hope so," she answered. "I'm really hungry and we should eat it before it gets cold. Let's dive in, shall we?" She knew without a doubt she was going to have a hard time trying to make him behave. She noticed his expression change from a smile to a frown as he began helping take the food to the table. It didn't matter one whit to her. *Is the poor little rich boy upset because he's not getting his way? I had a sneaking suspicion he had something else on his mind besides dinner.* She pretended to be oblivious to his intentions and took her time placing the food on the table. She even made a pot of coffee over his insistence that it was too hot for coffee. She informed him she'd fix a glass of iced tea for him. She watched him as he sat down on the swing on the veranda and with elbows propped on his knees, he began to crack his knuckles in an irritating manner glancing at her occasionally, as if he were trying to understand why she was as nonchalant as she seemed to be about their opportunity to be alone. She wished he'd turn the lights back on. The dimness made her uncomfortable.

When everything was ready they sat down together and began to eat. Rusty appeared to calm down after a while and soon was telling her about events of the day.

Suddenly, he turned his head, and cocked an ear toward the back-door. "Listen! Did you hear something?"

"What?" she asked. She had been listening to him, and had not heard anything out of the ordinary.

"That! Did you hear that?" He stood up, and walked to the door, and pushed it open to peer outside. "I wonder if one of the staff didn't close the gate as they left? That happened once before and we didn't know it until the next day."

At that instant all hell broke loose! There was a grunt, and then the deafening sound of the door being jerked off its hinges. Rusty was yelling for Kutzie to call the police, and then, two figures were suddenly scuffling, and the thud of a body hitting the floor was a sickening sound. It all happened so fast, Kutzie couldn't think! What was going on? Who was there?

"Rusty!" she screamed. "What is it?" And, at that moment, she saw what could be the bulk figure of Junior, with a knife flashing in his hand, and he lunged at Rusty. She saw only the outline shadow of a big person, but could not see where Rusty had gone.

Screaming, she ran inside for the gun!

Where had she left her handbag? She scrambled into the entry hall and saw it on the table by the front door. She was shaking so she could hardly get it opened, but she did and pulled out the gun at the exact second that Junior rushed at her, with eyes wide and mouth opened. She saw the grisly piece of what used to be a tongue in the middle of his mouth, twitching like the tongue of a snake, and she suddenly felt ill, like she was about to faint.

Pointing the gun at the face that was now only inches from her own, she squeezed the trigger as Ricky had taught her, and could have sworn she heard a sound come from Junior's throat. A groan. She watched him fall, and roll over on his face.

And, that was the last thing she remembered.

The room was a blur, and Kutzie had no idea where she was. It seemed she was in another world, because it was all too white. The movements she detected were white blurs. When she tried to raise up, a strong hand held her down. Where was she? What happened?

She did not realize she was asking the questions aloud. The room was spinning around.

A man's voice, low and soothing came from afar off, saying, "Miss Kline. You're in the hospital. Miss Kline . . ."

She put a hand to her forehead, tying to remember exactly what had happened. Was it all a nightmare? She remembered she and Rusty were eating supper on his veranda . . . As she recalled the memory, she screamed, holding the heels of her hands over her eyes. "No! Stop him! It's Junior! Junior's going to kill me! He's killing Rusty! NO! Leave us alone!" She screamed again and again. A nurse ran in and gave her an injection, saying, "Miss Kline, it's all right." And, before Kutzie passed out she heard the words, "She's suffering from shock."

When she came to the next time, the first words she heard were, "Miss Kline. Can you hear me Miss Kline? I'm Detective Jack Barker. Can you hear me?"

She nodded her head, with hands over her eyes to keep out the white light that was back.

"Can you remember what happened?" his gentle voice continued.

Silence. Then, "Junior was there! Junior came to Rusty's house! He attacked Rusty! Where is Rusty anyway? Is he all right?"

"What else? he prodded.

"And, then I ran to get my purse . . . The gun! I had the gun in my purse!" Her eyes were wild, opened wide at that moment and in a trembling voice she explained, "I had to buy a gun to scare Junior with. He kept following me everywhere I went, and Ricky said to buy a gun in order to protect myself. I told him I would never, ever use it. I told him I could never kill a human being. I never ever intended to shoot a gun. But, I thought I may have to scare him into thinking I would. When he chased me inside the house, I grabbed it and squeezed the trigger like Ricky taught me. I shot Junior in the face. I shot Junior. I shot a man." She moaned, and covered her eyes again, then, as an afterthought, asked, "How is Junior? Did I kill him! Did I?"

She could barely detect the detective's presence when he stood up and walked to the end of her bed. Everything was blurry! She did not know it was a sedative affecting her vision, as she strained and squinted her eyes trying to focus. She watched him walk back toward her, and sit down beside her on the bed. Taking her hand, he said again in a low voice,

"Right now, you're under arrest for murder, Miss Kline. Junior is dead. However, my own personal opinion is it was self-defense, but whenever the hospital releases you we will have to take you in. I think you should know there will be a trial and until then you're under arrest for murder."

She couldn't believe it! Kutzie Kline arrested for killing somebody? The person who had always vowed she could never harm an animal much less another human being?

She lay an arm across her face sobbing, and the detective walked away.

Someone else was in the room. Someone took her hand and it felt warm, and gentle. She opened her eyes and saw that it was Bill smiling down at her. "Oh, Bill. Darling!" spilled from her lips and she reached up to embrace him. He gathered her in his arms and held her tightly.

"Hey, better knock it off before someone sees you doing that." It was a woman's voice.

"Leona!" Kutzie cried, reaching for her and they embraced. "I didn't know you were here. How did you know I was here?"

"You must have had some of our business cards in your purse." Leona answered, and Bill nodded and added, "I think you had my number written on that little piece of scrap paper in your purse. I'm glad you didn't throw it away. Anyway, the police called both of us. I think the butler heard all the commotion, and dialed 911. I'm still in a fog myself about what actually happened."

"We were having supper . . . Rusty and I, on his veranda. Oh, yes, no one answered me awhile ago when I asked about Rusty. Where is he?"

She saw them look at each other, and felt Bill's hands tremble a little as he continued to hold hers. Leona shifted from one foot to the other. Kutzie felt a sense of foreboding. "Where is he?" she asked again raising her voice slightly . . .

"Junior killed him. Evidently, stabbed him with some kind of knife and Rusty bled to death!" Bill's eyes were full of sympathy.

"NO! NO!" She screamed. "NO!" Her wracking sobs shook her entire body and Bill held her closer against him. A nurse came running in with a needle, but when she rushed to Kutzie's side, Bill stopped her. "She doesn't need that." he told her. "She needs to be aware of what's going on. She can handle it. I want her out of this hospital anyway. She seems to be fine other than the emotional shock."

"She needs to released in someone's care," the nurse explained, "because she's been given a sedative and isn't able to drive. She's fine other than that."

"Since she's already had one shot, why were you about to give her another?" Bill asked.

"Just a mild one, because the other one is wearing off."

"Well, we'll be responsible for her." Bill said, and turning to Leona, he asked, "Why don't you help her get dressed while I run out and bring the car around?"

"I don't need any help!" Kutzie moaned. "Just hand me my clothes, please."

Another detective was sitting outside the door waiting, and as soon as they walked out of the hospital room, he snapped handcuffs on Kutzie's wrists and led her to his patrol car when they went outside, against a barrage of protests from both Bill and Leona. Kutzie never said a word. Bill seemed to go berserk! "What are you doing?" he asked, "We said we'd be responsible for Miss Kline. Where are you taking her?"

The officer looked as though he may take him in also. "To the police station, that's where. She's under arrest. I was under the impression she had been told she was under arrest."

"But, she isn't able to go to jail right now." Leona bellowed. "She's too weak!"

The officer looked at her with feigned pity, and put Kutzie into the patrol car and drove away, leaving them standing there with mouths open.

Atlanta had never seen a larger funeral, as the news of Rusty's untimely death, and, all the sordid story with all the details, was plastered across the front pages of the papers. Mail from all over America poured in to Kutzie, most praising her for the valor she showed in using the gun . . . shooting Junior before he killed her, as he had Rusty.

The next several weeks were a nightmare for Kutzie Kline. Charles and Lana, and Chris and Andrea flew in. When they learned that Rusty had made a new will only the week before, leaving everything he owned to Kutzie; the house, the store, his cars, even his bank account had been left to her, no one contested the will. The family felt that Rusty was an intelligent man and knew whom he wanted to leave his possessions to, and respected his wishes.

Because of the different ones who knew that Junior had been stalking Kutzie for weeks, the trial was speedy and the verdict was, 'not guilty'. Even Annie testified that when Kutzie came to her home that night because her car had stalled out, she had a feeling her son Junior, was behind it all especially when he had returned home shortly after and glared at Kutzie the way he had. Annie said she could see that Kutzie was a good girl and she had no hard feelings against her for shooting her son, because what else could she have done to protect herself? It was her testimony that had gone a long way in determining the verdict. Besides, the Hunt fortune went a long way also in convincing the jury that Kutzie was innocent. She had the best attorneys money could buy.

Amber and Richard were at the trial also, and when Kutzie was freed, the three of them went to the mansion with Charles, Lana, Chris and Andrea. Lana told Kutzie there were a few things she would like to have from the house if she had no objections, which of course, Kutzie didn't. Some belonged to Lana others only mementos. Chris wanted only some of the photos and memorabilia from their days at SMU, when Rusty played football.

When the Hunts all left to go to the airport and to their homes, Kutzie sat with her family in the den to discuss matters. "I can't believe all this belongs to you, Kootie." Amber said, as if in a trance. Kutzie shook her head. "I don't deserve it at all."

Richard smiled tiredly, "Baby, the man loved you very much. He wanted you to have it if anything should happen to him. Unfortunately it did. He had no one else to leave it to other than you. Enjoy it and remember him while you do."

"I can't believe his family didn't want it!" Kutzie exclaimed. "It's too much! This is a matter where millions of dollars are involved! How can they walk away and allow me to have it!"

"Because they love you, too. Because they have no use for it I suppose. Maybe the reason is because it's located where it is, maybe it's because it would complicate their lives. Whatever the reason they want you to have it because Rusty wanted you to. They respected their son's wishes more than most people do, it seems." her father smiled, and patted her hand.

Richard and Amber returned to Charlotte after only a few days in town, because Richard feared Melissa would miss him if he didn't show up at the nursing home after awhile. Kutzie wanted to go to Charlotte with them but had obligations in Atlanta that needed attention. Lana asked her to help with plans for Rusty's headstone because Rusty would want that. It was the hardest thing she had ever done. When Lana flew in from Dallas the next week they chose one before she flew off again.

During the next few days, Kutzie packed up, and moved into the mansion. She would have given her resignation at Elite, but Bill was there and she had to see him occasionally, though he had no idea she still felt as she did. *He probably thinks that whatever feelings I had for him before are gone. Oh, Bill, if you only knew . . .*

She could see his quizzical eyes on her many times during the day. He no doubt was trying hard not to crowd her into making any decisions about dating him. When he asked her to go to lunch she always refused. He had stopped calling her.

None of them at Elite knew that Rusty Hunt had left his fortune to her. That truth had not leaked out to the press so had been kept out of the papers. Kutzie told no one. Only her immediate family, and Rusty's family and their attorneys knew it and that was the way it was to stay.

In September, she had Brian drive her over to 313 Sycamore Street. She wanted to visit with Annie. The two women embraced, and Kutzie thanked her for her testimony on her behalf at the trial. Annie told her it was the least she could do especially since Junior had made her life a hell on earth since she had moved to Atlanta.

"Junior had no cause to do that to you. He was just mean, that's all. Just mean. I knew it."

"I'm sorry too, that your life was not any easier through the years." Kutzie told her sincerely. "I want to show my gratitude to you Annie, by giving you enough money to buy yourself a house in another neighborhood or to do whatever you need to do in order to make your life better. I brought this check over. It was given to me and I want to share it with you."

When Annie saw that the check was made out in the amount of $100,000, her eyes filled with tears. "I can't take this money. Thank you very much but I can't accept charity."

"Annie, listen to me. Do you know the meaning of the word 'charity'? It means 'love'. I want you to accept this out of love from me to you. It isn't because I feel sorry for you but because I want you to be able to do something for YOU for a change. Please? I really want you to have it. You have become the dearest friend in this town to me."

For an instant, Annie just looked at Kutzie and then, when she finally believed her she took the check from her fingers and with eyes spilling over with new tears, told Kutzie fondly, "I pray that the good Lord will bless you. You're an angel. Thank you." And, they embraced.

* * *

Kutzie had already begun to suspect something was wrong,

and made an appointment to see a doctor. He confirmed her suspicions that she was pregnant. He smiled when he told her she could expect the baby to make an appearance the last week of May. She was numb! How could that be? Thinking back, she recalled that she had made love with Rusty one day, and with Ricky the next. The baby could belong to either of them. She couldn't tell a soul.

She continued to go to work each morning, acting as if everything was exactly as it had always been. No one knew that she was a wealthy heiress nor had any idea that she had moved to the mansion for she kept her old telephone number and had simply forwarded it to the mansion so that when anyone called, they assumed she was at her old apartment. One of the attorneys had suggested she do that because no one need know that a young single woman such as she was, had suddenly come into such unbelievable wealth. There were a lot of greedy people in the world who would beat a path to her doorstep.

She kept the apartment even though she had moved out, but most of the furniture stayed. Since the lease was not yet up she kept it in case someone came along who needed a place to live. Of course, she would get Jan's permission in advance, before she allowed that to take place but one never knew when someone may need a place. Look at Annie. She should be in it rather than in her old house in that gosh-awful neighborhood.

Bill had asked her once or twice the month before to go to dinner, and she had been able to come up with fairly feasible excuses as to why she could not go, but lately he hadn't mentioned dinner or lunch or anything else and she wondered if perhaps he had detected her pregnancy. Because her stomach was growing bigger by the day she knew someone as observant as Bill, would detect the protrusion eventually.

She hadn't counted on the morning sickness and the secret was becoming extremely hard to keep. One day Bess walked into the rest room just after she had thrown up but Kutzie was still in the stall and Bess was never aware that she had puked her guts up. How long she could keep everyone from finding out, she was not sure but the clothes she had to wear did a good job of disguising the pregnancy.

Lana called often, but Kutzie could not bring herself to tell her that she was expecting Rusty's child because what if it was proven later to be Ricky's? Lana would surely take away all that Rusty had left her.

Even when Ricky called to ask her out she could not tell him either. He would definitely believe it was his baby, and it very well might be Rusty's. So she kept it her secret even when she and Ricky were out together, and when he caressed her as he kissed her goodnight she always held his hands so that he could not touch her tummy, even momentarily, by mistake. Also, she was careful not to stand against him while they kissed lest he detect the tummy bulge.

As the months passed, she and Bill seemed to be growing apart, because she was trying hard to keep him from finding out her secret and so she avoided him. It was so obvious that he thought she simply had no interest in him, and he in turn began to avoid her also not forcing his friendship on her in any way. Leona was so preoccupied with all the ads Elite was doing for Hubbard's, she acted as though it were her own personal project and kept to herself a lot, for which Kutzie was grateful. Bess was the one with the eagle eye and was always looking for something she could accuse Kutzie of. Even though Kutzie did not make it a point to go out of her way to avoid her nonetheless she tried not to cross paths with her.

Treva was busy learning a new job because she was up for the next promotion, and wanted to be a success at it and she was too busy to chat.

When Kutzie looked at Bill, he was always staring at her his eyes so sad she wanted to cry. She wanted to cuddle him and whisper that she loved him so very much but she knew she could never allow their love to develop into anything meaningful and continued to avoid direct contact with him. And, it broke her heart.

She even lost some weight, because she was not eating properly. Sometimes she went home for lunch and ate a bite or two of whatever the cooks prepared when she allowed them to fix a meal for her. Usually she went to the house and sat thinking about how she had allowed her life to become so messed up, until it was time to return to work.

* * *

One day, Amber called, to tell Kutzie that they were all disturbed over the fact that Melissa's breathing had changed. She said only that the nursing home sent her to the hospital in an ambulance. Kutzie said she would be on the next flight, and would rent a car and meet them at the hospital. When she arrived and raced into Melissa's room she scarcely knew her father. He was gaunt and extremely pale. How long since they last saw each other in Atlanta? Three months? Four? How time flies. Talking on the phone did not take the place of seeing each other, she realized with regret. She and Amber had talked more often than she and Richard, while planning Amber's Christmas Day wedding. Kutzie intended all along to pay for the wedding. It was something she had wanted to do, and besides, she knew that Richard had been out a lot with the expense of a nursing home, and, it would be a hardship for him to pay the wedding bill. Kutzie had started depositing several thousand dollars into his bank account occasionally during the past few weeks when he refused to accept money from her.

Her father was a proud man, and felt that what he earned was all he needed and would not touch the money she deposited in his account. Kutzie thought that if the expenses became too overwhelming, he would bend a little and use the money if he had to but he hadn't.

Chapter Seven

Devastating Anguish

Richard sat there staring into his beloved wife's face as she breathed with half-opened eyes that moved with each breath she took. It was apparent to anyone who saw him that his heart was breaking. He was oblivious to Kutzie and Amber's presence as well as the doctors and nurses entering the room.

Other relatives began arriving throughout the day from everywhere, especially from the south. There was a couple of cousins that came in from Little Rock and her dad's half-brother flew in from Nashville. Another brother came in from Charleston, South Carolina later in the day.

All were gathered around Melissa's bedside when she simply stopped breathing. When a nurse checked her blood pressure she quietly told them that Melissa had expired, and Richard broke down. He cried until both girls became extremely concerned, for he exhausted himself and seemed to have trouble with his breathing. When a doctor came in and examined him he informed the girls that their father should be hospitalized and Richard was given a strong sedative immediately. As Kutzie and Amber stood beside his bed Kutzie thought back to all that happened during the last several months, and found it hard to comprehend all that had transpired. Unbelievable happenings. She finally dragged herself away, telling Amber she was going to the funeral home to make Melissa's final arrangements.

At the home, she learned that Richard had already taken care of not only Melissa's, but also his own funeral arrangements years ago.

The baby inside her was kicking so she could hardly sit comfortably while driving back to her Dad's house. Amber was there waiting, and she and Kutzie cried together arms around each other. Kutzie felt compelled to confide in her that she was pregnant and that night the two of them sat up until after midnight talking and Kutzie finally told her. She didn't mention that the baby could be another man's, only that she and Rusty had weakened once in a moment of passion. Amber seemed to understand, assuring her sister that she was there for her no matter what.

The funeral took place on an unusually warm day for December, and Kutzie thought she was for sure going to pass out from the heat. Richard was still hospitalized, but the doctors had said they may release him the next day, but he was not strong enough to attend his wife's funeral over his extreme resistance. Amber and Kutzie managed to convince him that the doctors were right. Because of his weakened condition he gave up arguing . . . he was too exhausted.

Kutzie had talked to Leona a couple of times while in Charlotte. Once to tell her of her mother's death. Elite had sent flowers. And then, Kutzie called later to talk about how her father was told he could not attend her funeral because of his condition. She hoped each time that Bill would be the one to answer the phone when she called, and longed to ask Leona about him, but she was being cautious about revealing her overwhelming love for him at the moment. Leona did not mention his name. She asked that Kutzie continue to keep in touch and said they all missed her and that was about the extent of their conversation.

Amber came over to the house every day to be with Kutzie while she was still in town, and they talked of Amber and Randy's wedding plans. Kutzie wanted them to go house-hunting, which was to be a wedding present from her. She wanted them to find a home they wanted, and she would do the rest.

Christmas Day was not a big event because it was Christmas but because it was Amber and Randy's wedding day. The bride was beautiful in her white chantilly lace gown, with her long dark-brown hair flowing to her waist. Randy was a handsome groom in his white tux standing beside her. It seemed everyone in town was there, and all seemed to be enjoying themselves. They left for Hawaii for a week's honeymoon.

Kutzie wondered if her father had noticed her slight weight gain and assumed he hadn't. At least, he hadn't said anything, and until he did, she had no intentions of bringing up the subject. She was going to return to Atlanta in a day or two anyway, and saw no reason to say anything unless he took her up on her invitation to go with her, and stay with her awhile. He didn't, and she left him alone, reluctantly.

* * *

Back in Atlanta, Kutzie enjoyed preparing a nursery, and did not return to Elite for several days although she ached to see Bill, and day-dreamed about what she would say to him one day in the near future.

She fantasized that they would work everything out once she told him she was carrying a baby she did not know who the father was, and he would tell her it made no difference, that he loved her anyway.

Her doctor sensed that something was bothering her and was concerned because she was not eating properly. He warned her that unless she ate more nutritionally, the baby would be underweight, and under-developed. He advised her to stop worrying about whatever was bothering her.

* * *

One day while shopping at the store for maternity clothes, she bought a book of names for babies. She had not been into Hubbard's recently, lest some of the old employees would detect her pregnancy, but no one seemed to notice because she made it a point not to see several of them who knew her.

That evening, she pored over the different names in the book, saying each aloud to see which sounded best. She decided that if it were a girl, she would be named 'Jessica', if a boy, he would be 'Chase'.

The next week she returned to work, and when she drove into the garage she saw Bill parking his car as she parked hers. It was not until he was out of his automobile, and was walking toward the entrance into Elite that he saw her, and stopped in his tracks. He looked so good to her as he stood there, tall and good-looking, staring as though he could not believe she was there, although she didn't understand why he should be surprised; after all, she worked there even if she hadn't been there in awhile.

"How are you, Kutzie?" he asked hesitantly, his gaze sweeping over every feature of her face . . .

"Fine, Bill. And you?"

"I'm not worth a dime anymore. I can't think, and I can't eat, nor sleep because I'm thinking of you night and day." Same old honest Bill, blurting out the truth in his first sentence although she was surprised when she heard the words, even though he was up-front about everything. She was struck by his integrity again, as she had been many times in the past.

Her heart lurched in her chest. She dropped her head staring at the walkway, as they slowly made their way into the building, because she could not bear to look at him.

He stepped in front of her and stopped, so that she could go no farther and asked, "What's going on? Why are you avoiding me? Kutzie, as much as I need you and you need me how can you avoid me? All that you had to go through back in August, and now you've lost your mom and your dad's sick. How much more can you go through without someone by your side, who loves you as much as I do?"

"Oh, Bill!" she cried with emotion. And stood on tiptoe to take his face between her palms, and then began smothering it with kisses as she threw both arms around his neck, embracing him with every fiber of strength she had. He responded in like manner, and they could not hold each other tight enough nor get close enough. He squeezed her so tightly she practically gasped for breath, and didn't mind at all. The two of them stood there kissing each other's face, laughing and crying together with their arms enfolded around each other. Kutzie stepped back laughing as she smoothed her hair, saying, "I must look a wreck! Look at me! Is my lipstick smeared?"

He laughed, and gathered her in his arms again. "You don't have on any lipstick, darling. I've kissed it all off. But, you look good to me regardless of lipstick, mussy hair, whatever."

She pushed him back gently and whispered, "Oh, Bill. We shouldn't have done this. I've tried so hard to get you out of my system and now this . . . this . . . reunion? Whatever . . . it is we have to forget each other. I don't want you to hate me." She buried her face into his suit lapel as she said it.

"What are you talking about, sweetheart? Hate you? For what? I couldn't hate you for anything in this world. You could never do anything that would cause me to hate you. What's going on with you?" He looked puzzled. Did he not feel her tummy?

"I'm . . . Oh, never mind . . . Let's go inside, shall we? I need to go to the Ladies room, and comb my hair, and re-apply lipstick."

"Don't you think you should tell me what it is that's bothering you first?" he asked, holding her head against his chest.

"I'll tell you later, okay?" she promised.

"Why don't I come by your apartment tonight, so we can talk?" he asked, smiling, stroking her hair lovingly.

She fumbled with his lapel momentarily, before she finally said, "I don't live there anymore, Bill. I've moved into Rusty Hunt's house."

"You have? Since when? Who's staying with you?" he asked, obviously jolted by the unexpected announcement. "I guess that explains why I never see your car parked in your space. I've driven over to your apartment several times."

"I live alone. Rusty gave the house to me. He left it to me in his will. And, you remember he gave me that Cadillac? Was that the car you looked for or had you forgotten that?"

"No, I hadn't forgotten about your having the Cadillac. But, he willed his home to you? Well, I'll be darn. I can't even imagine his doing that. How about that! Pretty damn generous of the guy, I guess, especially since you weren't married to him. He must've loved you a lot!"

"You've seen the house then?"

"Only in the Sunday Magazine that comes with the Sunday paper. There was a spread in it once about his mansion. Fourteen rooms, six bathrooms, plus all the other extras, right?"

She nodded. "You're welcome to come by and visit anytime, Bill"

"I suppose he left it to you because y'all were engaged to be married and he wanted you to have it in the event anything should happen to him?" Bill made the statement rather than asked a question, because it seemed to bother him. She wondered why. She postulated that perhaps she owed him an explanation.

"His folks wanted me to have it although I thought for sure they would contest the will. They didn't. They said Rusty had a mind of his own and if he wanted me to have it, so did they."

He shook his head. "Amazing people. Truly amazing, generous people. How have we been reaching you, when we call your old phone number? Apparently you have a different one, being in a different area? The house in in Buckhead, isn't it?"

She looked up into his eyes, her own limpid and innocent. "My telephone is forwarded to the mansion. I still have the apartment and it has most of my old furniture in it, still." She tried to smile. "Bill . . . I'm . . . uh . . ."

He waited, watching her lips as she stood there pondering how she should tell him. "What . . . ?" he prodded.

She simply shook her head and walked into the building, looking back over her shoulder at him, calling, "I'll call you later, Gator." She turned it into a joke so he wouldn't think it was something serious. He ran and caught up with her and spun her around and kissed her one more time. She melted in his strong gentle arms a fleeting moment, then broke away and went into the Ladies' Room. She fell against the door when it closed and looked up toward heaven. "Thank You." She said aloud, feeling warm inside at the thought that Bill still loved her and would when she told him she was carrying a baby that belonged to another man.

It was a normal day at Elite. Bess running around trying to get someone to tell her how to do a project, Treva chewing her gum and smiling, while she performed her duties wholeheartedly. Leona sitting at the computer, with her face screwed up like always. Mr. Shaw poring over How-To books, Kutzie sketching ads, and Bill talking on the telephone to prospective customers, while stretching his neck throughout the day to see where Kutzie was.

When noon arrived, he ran to her office and asked

nonchalantly if she cared to have lunch with him. She had wondered already if she would accept if he were to ask, but the baby inside her had been unusually active throughout the morning, and she wasn't sure if she should. But, oh, how she longed to go . . .

She looked into his pleading eyes and could not refuse. She needed nourishment and should go to a good restaurant where there was a good selection. She nodded, happy to accept his invitation.

They drove to Roswell which was about twenty miles from Atlanta, because Bill said he wanted her to see The North Fulton area during Christmas. The decorations were something else and would be taken down in a day or two. He said he especially wanted her to see Bulloch Hall, where President Teddy Roosevelt's mother lived once upon a time.

I don't care where somebody used to live . . . I only want to be with you in a secluded spot.

However, she determined that it was a beautiful area and worth seeing after all, and she was also impressed with the mall with its boutiques, and restaurants. It was a wonderful day!

They overstayed their lunch hour some, but Bill and Kutzie both were so bubbly with happiness at being together, they didn't care if Leona got angry. Once in awhile the thought came to Kutzie's mind about her pregnancy, and she remembered that he must never know. Not yet.

Since she did not know who the baby's father was, it had to remain her secret. She would have to make plans to leave Atlanta soon . . . very soon . . . and, have her baby. Later, she could say she had adopted it while she was in . . . where? . . . Dallas, Texas! Her mind whirled, as Bill raced back to Atlanta hoping to make it to Elite before Leona became too upset when she missed them.

Bess spotted them as they walked in. "Well, it's about time." she jeered. "I tell you, Kutzie, you can't leave men alone can you?"

Kutzie stopped in her tracks directly in front of Bess, and stood there. "I wasn't aware that I had to or that it was anyone's business if I do or don't."

"What time did you two leave here?" Leona called from her office, mumbling because she was holding a pencil between her lips.

"A little after 12:00." Bill answered honestly.

"Well, it's 1:30 now. Where did you two go anyway? Was it lunch only or did you have to stop somewhere on business?" Leona quizzed.

"It was lunch only. I took Kutzie to Bullock Hall for lunch, and the traffic was heavier than I expected it to be." Bill said truthfully, and Kutzie once again was awed by his integrity.

Why wasn't she more honest as he was? One day in the future, after she'd had the baby and after she told him it was adopted she would be completely honest.

What would he think if he found out she had lied about the baby one day in the future?

Well, he wouldn't find out. How could he? She would hire a shyster attorney to draw up adoption papers if she had to. How was that for real dishonesty, she shuddered at the thought, that she was a terrible person these days.

* * *

New Year's Eve Kutzie went to bed at 9:00 p.m. The next morning, she awoke feeling sick to her stomach, and she ran into the bathroom, retching. After she had eaten breakfast she went into the Study, and lay on the velvet settee, thinking what the baby would look like if it were Ricky's. And, what it would look like if it were Rusty's. Well, Rusty was an absolute doll. Other than Bill, he was the most handsome man she had ever seen in her life. But Ricky was cute. He had pretty eyes anyway. She fantasized about the baby having Ricky's eyes, Rusty's mouth, Bill's teeth, and her hair. She was already anxious to get the pregnancy over with!

January through March she stayed home a lot. She worried about her father being alone now, but he seemed to be feeling all right, so she waited until it was almost time for the baby to be born before she made definite plans to stay with him a few weeks. Because she had taken a leave of absence from Elite, she seldom talked to anyone there anymore. When they called she sometimes let the answering machine pick it up, or else asked Rodney to find out who it was. She didn't mind speaking to any of her friends if she felt like it, but it was a rarity anymore that she felt like conversing with anyone for any length of time. Besides, they may suspect something and if they asked what would she tell them?

She worried constantly about whether people would later on be able to look at the baby, and see that he resembled Ricky or Rusty. If it were a girl perhaps no one could see any resemblance whatsoever to either of the men for she would look exactly like her. She smiled, thinking that it was drawing near to the time she should pack several bags, and go to Charlotte and stay until the baby was at least a month old. She surely would have lost all the weight she was gaining, by that time.

She looked at the calendar. Easter was only two days away. She and Amber planned to have dinner together at their father's house, and Kutzie had her bags packed to drive over to Charlotte the next day. She called Elite, telling Leona and the rest of the gang there that she was going to be in Charlotte for a few days.

Bill called the night before she left and asked if she would like to go to dinner and to a movie afterwards. She said she didn't care to. "Kutzie, you've been avoiding me again. Why? Did I do anything to make you mad at me? If I did I wasn't aware of it, because God knows I would never in a million years knowingly hurt you, nor even make you mad, if I could help it."

She laughed. "You haven't done a thing wrong, darling. I've had a bug, and I may be contagious. I'm going to Charlotte and visit for a few days." That was an out-and-out lie, for she had no intentions of returning before June. "I need to check on my family," which was true.

Because she was showing by that time she had bought larger sized clothing, glad that loose-fitting clothes were the style, because she could no longer hide her bulging tummy very well, and that was why she should not see Bill although she desired to so much!

"I would love to come over, Kutzie. May I?"

"I'm sorry, Bill, but no. Just remember though that whatever happens, I love you. I always will. Don't be angry with me darling. Don't give up on me if you don't hear from me for awhile." And, saying that, she hung up the phone, and then took the receiver off the hook.

* * *

The gray clouds were rolling and the wind chilly when she drove out I-85 early in the morning. Kutzie was all wrapped up in her fake fur jacket. She refused to wear real fur because she did not believe in killing the animals. She had even insisted that Lana take her fur coats out of the coat closet when she was moving out her things, even though Lana said she rarely wore furs in Dallas because it didn't get cold enough there and she'd rather leave them because Atlanta did sometimes get cold. But, Kutzie insisted because the thought of the slain animals bothered her. The fake one Kutzie wore was a rare beauty, and she enjoyed wearing it while she was pregnant because it fit her swelling body comfortably.

The weather seemed cold by Atlanta's standards, but after all, April sometimes was a cold month. A new front had moved through, and the temperature had plummeted during the night. At least, warmer weather was predicted to arrive in the next two or three days, hopefully by her birthday, which was only two days away, the day after Easter.

* * *

At her father's, she took her things to her old bedroom and hung her clothes. Some were maternity, but most were to wear after the baby arrived. Even though her father had to see that she was pregnant she could not bear to tell him voluntarily, and wore her loosest shirts trying to hide her prominent stomach from him and her friends. It was especially hard on April 21st, her birthday, when certain friends, and family members called, and dropped by, bringing little gifts to her, but she thought she managed fairly well.

One evening, while Kutzie and her father sat talking about the day's events, a sudden pain gripped Kutzie across the back, and she screamed. Her father showed no surprise when he heard it. He simply walked to the telephone, and dialed 911.

* * *

Kutzie was fighting to wake up but it was too much of an effort, and she drifted once again into the blessed state of unconsciousness.

"Koots, it's a boy! Wake up, and see your beautiful baby boy."

To Kutzie, Amber seemed surrounded by heavy fog when she opened her eyes and saw her sister's face only inches from her own. That was all she remembered for she blacked out again. The next thing she knew, she heard the sound of voices in her room, and when she opened her eyes and looked around her doctor was standing beside her bed, smiling down at her. "Well, Mrs. Kline, I thought you were going to sleep all day. You remember that you gave birth to a son this morning, don't you?" *MRS. Kline? This doctor thinks I'm married, and that's my married name?*

No, she didn't remember giving birth. The last thing she remembered was flying along in the rear of an ambulance with a man dressed in white taking her blood pressure, while she suffered unbearable pain. And, then she must have blacked out for she had no recollection of anything else.

"The baby's drinking a bottle of sugared water right at this moment, but the nurse is going to bring him to you in a few minutes."

"Thank you." She mumbled. "Where's my family?"

The doctor turned to the nurse standing on the other side of Kutzie's bed. "Did her folks leave?"

She shook her head. "No, they said they were going downstairs to get a bite to eat in the cafeteria. It looked to them as if Mrs. Kline was going to sleep the day away."

She and the doctor laughed, but Kutzie wished they would go away, and leave her alone. It was not a time for laughing and talking. She hurt all over. Besides, she wanted to see her new baby and see if he looked like his father. When they lay her baby boy beside her, tears filled her eyes as she gazed down at him lovingly. The first thing she noticed was the dimples. The baby was Rusty's, there was no doubt. She kissed his cheek again and again, and the baby stirred, opening his mouth and nuzzling against her bosom. She had not decided on whether or not to breast-feed, even though her doctor had encouraged it. At this moment it seemed the most natural thing in the world for her to put the baby to her breast, and instinctively he began to suck. As he nursed, she smoothed the dark, ample head of hair, and ran her fingertips along the direction of his brow-line.

When her family walked in they realized that what they saw at that moment was the instant bonding of mother and child and it was such a touching scene, Amber cried. Kutzie looked up when she heard the sobs, and motioned for them to come to her bedside, where she hugged them both watching Richard's eyes for a sign of disapproval. There was none detected. Just a love shining in his eyes that Kutzie recognized as forgiveness for whatever wrong she may have done.

Chapter Eight

The Kidnapping

Kutzie settled down into her old room when she and the baby went to her father's home upon their release from the hospital. It was temporarily a combination nursery and adult bedroom. Not at all what she had waiting at her home in Atlanta, where there was a fully furnished nursery, and her own lavishly furnished room consisting of a king-sized bed with its flowing, lacy canopy. Still, she was happy in the old room with all its memories, and she wondered how she had gotten herself into such a predicament recently. She was actually hiding out like a criminal! Hiding from her friends including Bill. Oh, how she longed to see him but when certain thoughts entered her mind, she felt a twinge of guilt and distress recognizing they would probably never see each other again. Her vow to herself that she would not break his heart by allowing him to find out she had been intimate with Rusty Hunt and also Ricky Larson when he thought she was so pure and innocent was for keeps. So she settled down to keeping her father well-fed, and happy.

* * *

Amber and Randy were doing well. Occasionally, Kutzie went to visit, helping Amber decorate her new home.

One day a letter came with an Atlanta postmark.

It was from Bill.

She tore it open in eager anticipation, and read:

"Dear Kutzie,

All of us here at Elite are wondering about you. It seems no one has heard from you in several weeks, and we're worried. I keep telling myself that no news is good news, but in this case, I don't think that old cliché fits. If you are well and your family is well, you would stay in touch with some of us, and I know that. If you receive this letter please contact one of us to let us know how you are. Please, Kutzie! Remember what I told you? I meant every word!

Much love . . . always!
Bill

She sat holding the letter in her shaking hands, holding back the tears of desire to see him and walked over to Chase's bassinet, and looked down at him sleeping soundly without a care in the world. *Chase, darling, if you only knew how much I love you and that because of you I'm abandoning my true love so he will never find out about you.* She leaned over and kissed his fat little face searching the features as she always did, for some sort of clue as to which man he resembled that she might recognize. She was not completely convinced that the dimples were a sure sign that Rusty was the father, for the baby's eyes were a deep blue like Ricky's.

Kutzie, with letter in hand walked into the living room to say something to her father who sat in his recliner peacefully. She sat down beside him in her mother's old chair, and re-read Bill's letter. She smiled to herself. *Perhaps our paths will cross another day, Darling, and if they should I'll treasure the moment!*

It was nearly noon when she finally went into the kitchen to fix a bite of lunch for Richard and herself, because he was sleeping so soundly, it looked as though she would have to cook the meal first, and then wake him to eat it.

When it was ready and on the table she pondered on whether she should wake him knowing he had not been feeling too well and seemed so tired too often but he should eat a good, nourishing meal, too.

When she touched his shoulder, she saw that his eyes were open. "Oh, Dad. I thought you were still asleep. Lunch is on the table."

When he made no movement, she knelt beside his chair and touched his face. It was cold! Clammy cold! And the eyes continued to stare into space. She screamed. Almost as soon as the scream came out of her mouth she regained her composure and calmed down because Chase was sleeping in the next room. She had to find out what was wrong with her dad!

But she knew. She could sense that the cold, clammy skin was death. He had died in his sleep apparently, but when? How long ago? That morning? She had not even checked on him since she woke up. But, he was alive then because he said 'good morning' to her. *Oh, Daddy, why didn't you say you weren't feeling well so I could have taken you to a doctor?*

She ran to the telephone, and dialed 911, then called Amber at her job. Amber took the news amazingly well when Kutzie told her kindly and calmly that she wasn't sure if Daddy was breathing or not, and that she was waiting on an ambulance to arrive.

Amber skidded into a parking space almost simultaneously with the ambulance. Kutzie scampered out when the rear door of the ambulance swung open, holding little Chase against her bosom.

Richard was pushed inside into the emergency room, and the nurses and doctors rushed to his side hovering around him. Then, hurriedly took him into surgery, although Kutzie knew he was definitely dead.

In what seemed like hours rather than the minutes it actually was, a doctor walked out to break the sad news to Richard's daughters that he was brought in with no vital signs, and they were unable to revive him. Kutzie swayed and screamed, and Amber snatched Chase from her arms, pacifying the baby when he began to cry.

Kutzie was moaning in her grief. How could she bear losing her father so soon after her mother's death, and after losing Bill and Rusty too? Amber seemed to be the brave one as she coaxed her older sister to snap back and remember she had a son who needed her and told her that death was a part of life. Kutzie stared at Amber when she said that, and nodding her head she hugged her, and thanked her for reminding her of that.

It was true what Amber said about the responsibility Kutzie had to her baby but it was a sad thing that their father died without getting to know his first grandson. Richard was not elderly, but he had lost so much when he lost Melissa and the will to live was a part of that loss.

As they sat in the emergency room hugging and consoling each other, Kutzie felt a hand on her shoulder and she turned to see an old friend from the past standing over them, with a big smile across her face. It was the friend she had "lost" the intern to that she had told Rusty about . . . the one who wanted to marry her until she introduced him to a friend, the friend standing there now in the emergency room grinning down at her.

Kutzie managed a feeble smile, wiping her eyes with her fingertips and half-heartedly hugging the woman, Crystal, who asked, "What in the world are you doing here in the emergency room?"

"Dad was just pronounced dead apparently from a heart attack." Kutzie answered, digging through her handbag searching for a tissue, and wiping her eyes when she found one.

Crystal looked stricken, "Oh, Kutzie honey, I'm so sorry." Then in the next breath, asked, "Is this your baby? What a doll! Boy or girl?"

Kutzie straightened her shoulders and removed the blanket from Chase's top half to show him off. "A boy. His name is Chase. And, yes he belongs to me."

"I heard through the grapevine last year, that you were engaged. That was the last I heard. Who was the guy? When did you marry?" Crystal queried, and Kutzie squirmed.

"His name was Rusty Hunt." was all she said, and Crystal gushed, "Oh, yeah. I knew it was a bigwig, but I had forgotten his name. Does the baby look like his daddy?"

"Dimples and all." She answered. And shifting Chase to the other knee, asked, "What about you? I've thought about you and Coy, and wondered where you were these days? Is he still working here at the hospital or did he open his own offices?"

The woman fidgeted, and twisted her fingers, almost as though she were angry, and finally answered, "We're no longer together. He turned into a drug addict and I divorced him."

The news shocked Kutzie, and the roles reversed themselves when Kutzie offered her sympathy to her life-long school chum. "I'm sorry. I didn't know. Do you have any children?"

Crystal seemed to be really angry then, and her face began to twitch. She answered through gritted teeth, "I lost a baby son recently. Meningitis."

"Meningitis?" Kutzie echoed. "I read about it in the papers, I think. I just didn't connect the name . . . Parretti . . . Oh, Crystal, I'm so sorry."

Crystal smiled lightly, "Thanks. Life deals a low blow sometimes, doesn't it?"

Amber, who had not said anything before then, spoke up. "We have to take the good with the bad. If life were a bed of roses all the time we would never learn to appreciate what we have."

Kutzie patted Amber's knee. "Good philosophy, Sis." And, turned back to Crystal when the woman asked, "Do y'all still live at the same place? I'd like to help in any way I can knowing you have a lot to do, arranging your dad's funeral and all. Maybe I can baby-sit while you make the arrangements?"

The gesture moved Kutzie. "Dad's arrangements are made already, because he made them himself. What we do need to do however, is make some phone calls. We need to notify the funeral home, and all of our relatives."

"Would you like me to drop by later and keep an eye on the baby, or help with anything else?" Crystal offered.

Kutzie, knowing her friend must really want to help told her yes, she would appreciate that.

The doctor returned and told the girls that it appeared that Richard's heart had simply stopped beating, and therefore an autopsy would not be necessary, unless they wanted one for their own satisfaction. They agreed that it would not be necessary. The doctor said he would call the funeral home, and that they should go home and rest awhile. The grim task of notifying those same relatives they had to call when their mom passed away began as soon as they reached the house. Crystal came over shortly after and took over the liability of little Chase immediately. Kutzie smiled as she watched her hug Chase lovingly.

* * *

During the funeral, Kutzie sat with relatives in the area designated, while Crystal tended to Chase on the back row in the chapel in the event he should cry she could step outside and quiet him without disturbing the services. The chapel was filled to capacity, and some had to stand outside, because there was no room for them to sit down. Richard had many friends from all over the area, including former customers and business associates.

When the services ended, and the directors led the mourners outside to their cars for the procession to the cemetery, Kutzie stood at the doorway watching for Crystal. When she didn't spot her she stepped inside the Family limousine that was waiting on her, and sat beside Amber. "I didn't see Crystal," she whispered. "She may have left the chapel already because Chase was fretting, but I wonder where she could have gone?"

"She and the baby could be in this crowd anywhere and you wouldn't see them." Amber answered. "She may be waiting in the ladies lounge because there is a nice big couch in there."

Kutzie nodded, looking to see if any breast milk had leaked through her blouse for it was feeding time and her breasts were sore and swollen with the abundant milk supply she possessed.

After the burial service, Kutzie and Amber hung around the funeral home waiting on Crystal, but she was nowhere to be found. Kutzie had already begun to be concerned until Amber commented that more than likely she had taken the baby to their home, and was waiting for them there because she had not been able to find Kutzie in the throng at the funeral home. Still, the nagging thought Kutzie had was that she had been among family members at all times, and should have been easy enough to spot . . . unless the baby was crying, and she didn't want to bother her. And, he probably was beginning to cry as he became hungry, because the services had lasted longer than planned.

They didn't see Crystal's automobile parked out front as they drove into the garage at the house, although many other cars were parked in the drive, and along the curb up and down the block. Food from friends and neighbors who had prepared it and brought it over, was waiting for them when they went inside. Kutzie wasn't hungry. In fact, she was very uncomfortable when she had to go into the bathroom to pad her bra with wash cloths so the milk would not leak through. As she sat down at the dining table she whispered to Amber, "I'm really worried. I wonder where she could be?"

"I'm worried, too, Kootie. I'm kind of suspicious of that friend of yours but I wasn't going to say anything." Amber mumbled.

"What do you mean?" Kutzie asked. She didn't like the tone she detected in Amber's voice.

"I don't know exactly. I remember when y'all were in school together, Mom never did like her because she thought Crystal was a sneaky child. Remember?"

"No, not really, but she and I were never close. She was the type who was jealous of my other friends. But when I worked at the hospital as a volunteer, she was a patient there for over a week, and I visited her almost every day. She was very nice. We had lots of long talks about school, and the people we went to school with. She ran around with a different group of kids than I did and I think that's why I never knew her too well in elementary school, then she dropped out of high school and we didn't see each other anymore until she came in as a patient that day at the hospital." As Kutzie talked she stared into space musing on the past.

It was late in the day before the last friend left their house and the relatives had all gone to a hotel, even though the two girls tried to talk certain ones into staying the night there at their home. Kutzie was frantic by nightfall because Crystal had not so much as called.

She had to call the police and report that the baby had been kidnapped, for obviously Crystal was not going to bring him home. She worried that she may have had an accident and if that were the case, the police would know that.

After she called and the police were on their way out to talk to her and to get some sort of photo of the baby and other information, Kutzie fell apart. She had reached a point where she felt she could not cope with all that had happened. The strain was too much for her. Amber consoled her as best she could but Kutzie sat in a crumpled heap on the end of the sofa, crying her heart out in overwhelming grief.

Amber went into Kutzie's bedroom and found the baby-book the hospital had provided which contained the baby's footprints, and the photo taken of him soon after his birth. She also, had taken pictures with her Polaroid during the weeks since the baby's birth, and she gathered it all together for the police and went back downstairs. There was a knock on the door as she returned to the living room and when she opened it, she invited the police officers inside. Kutzie saw them come in and began to ramble about Crystal taking her baby away, at the time of her daddy's funeral, which was so soon after their mother's death, which closely followed the death of the baby's father. It was plain that the officers felt a sense of pity but Amber wondered if it was because of the loss of the loved ones, or because of the condition Kutzie was in. She looked like some other person, rather than the beauty she had always been. Her eyes were swollen, and her face tear-streaked, and makeup had run down her cheeks. Her hair was tangled and her clothes wrinkled as though she had slept in them. Amber was almost ashamed of her yet she felt she understood the heart-ache she was undergoing, obviously not caring what she looked like. She whispered to Kutzie that she would give the officers all the information they needed, if she would like to lie down awhile but Kutzie spun around and abruptly threw herself on the sofa, covering her face with both hands, crying, "I can't rest. I want my baby! Please find my baby! Please call Ricky, Amber. Please?"

"Who is Ricky?" one of the officers asked, and Amber shrugged her shoulders for she evidently did not remember hearing the name before.

The policemen assured the two women they would do their best to track down the baby's kidnapper, and left the house. Amber, almost impatiently, turned to Kutzie. "Okay who is this Ricky person and how do I contact him and why?"

"He's the police officer I met in Atlanta. Remember when you and Dad brought the furniture to me the next day after I left here to take that job in Atlanta and I told y'all about almost getting a ticket for speeding while on my way to the apartment from the hotel? Well, the officer and I have gotten to be pretty good friends. We've dated a few times. I told you about him, didn't I? He might want to help, because he would take a personal interest in the case. You know?" *He certainly might take a personal interest in the situation . . .*

Amber smiled, albeit a little sadly. "Great idea, Koot. We need all the help we can get. How do I reach him? Ya got his number?"

"Yes. Just a minute." And, she forced herself to push her body off the sofa, and dragged herself upstairs to her bedroom. She came down moments later clutching an address book in her hand, and handed it to Amber who moved to the telephone, and dialed the number. While it rang she asked Kutzie, "Would you rather talk to him?" And, before Kutzie could answer, she heard the 'hello' on the other end of the line.

"Ricky Larson, please." Amber said.

"This is he."

"Mr. Larson, this is Kutzie Kline's sister, Amber, and I . . ."

"Kutzie's sister?" His voice came loudly across the line, almost breaking Amber's ear drums. "Good God, is anything wrong with Kutzie? Where in hell is she?"

"She's right here beside me. She would like for you to come to Charlotte to help with a problem at your earliest convenience, if it's at all possible."

"Give me the directions. I'll be there as soon as I can call in to the station, and take some time off."

When Amber hung up she dropped beside Kutzie on the sofa, smiling, "That guy must like you a lot! All I had to say was that you needed him to come here to Charlotte. I figured you don't feel like talking to anybody right now and can explain things better in person, right? Besides, if he's here he can start helping us look for that creep, Crystal. I wish I could get my hands on her right now." she stood up, and walked back to the phone. "I guess I'd better call Randy and let him know she still hasn't returned with the baby, so I'll be here awhile longer."

Kutzie nodded, wiping her eyes. "I hate for you to be away from Randy like this, Amber. Ricky is a very good friend. Perhaps he can help us find Crystal and Chase. Oh, Amber, it scares me to think what could happen to little Chase. I wonder if Crystal knows how to care for a little baby?"

"I don't know. But, Kootie, we can't stay up all night. What are you going to do? The police said you should stay close to the telephone and if they hear anything they'll call immediately. But, I feel like we should be doing something! Don't you?"

"Yes! I'm going crazy, Amber. I can't stand this waiting, waiting, waiting! Oh, God, what should I DO?" She jumped up and began pacing, tears streaming.

She was huddled in a corner of the sofa when the knock on the door aroused her from drifting in and out of sleep. As though she were in another world, she struggled to grasp her surroundings and stumbled to the door. She started to open it when she snapped to and called hoarsely, "Who is it?"

"It's Ricky."

She hurriedly unlocked the door and pushed it open and he walked in and hugged her tightly. "What's wrong? Your sis called to say you needed me."

"It's a long story, Ricky. Please sit down and I'll try to tell you, and hope it all makes sense to you."

It took awhile to explain it all; the pregnancy, the birth, her father's untimely death, Crystal, and the kidnapping. When she finished talking, Ricky simply sat there with mouth opened, staring at her. The first words that came out of his mouth was, "The baby's mine?"

"No. Rusty's."

"How old is the baby?"

"He's three weeks old."

She could see the wheels turning inside his head, and then he seemed satisfied with her answer. She had not bothered to tell him that the baby had arrived a month early so his calculations were regarding a full-term baby, and that meant that he must remember exactly when they had been together. He had a stern look on his face and she was unable to determine whether he was angry with her or concerned that the baby was kidnapped, or both. She asked him what was wrong and was he angry or disappointed in her?

He held her hands in his. "My poor baby. You've been through so very much. I can't be either angry or disappointed in you. Look at all that has happened to you this past year and I know that you're not the type to sleep around. A cop knows that. Getting pregnant was probably the result of a terrible mistake, right?"

"Rusty Hunt and I were engaged to be married, you remember, I told you? We made one mistake one time. That's all it takes, I guess."

He wrapped his arms about her just as Amber entered the room. She looked shocked when she saw her sister in the arms of this strange man and she whirled around and ran upstairs to her room. Kutzie had not seen her there, but Ricky did. However he said nothing. He stood up and walked to the telephone and dialed the police department. His voice was so low Kutzie was unable to make out what he said, but when he hung up he went back to sit beside her once again and put his arm around her shoulder. "I want you to get all the rest you can. We're going to fly to San Francisco tomorrow morning. I'm going to call the airlines right now and make our reservations. There's a woman matching Crystal's description who's in jail in 'Frisco, and a police officer was about to call you and ask if you'd like to fly out there and identify her first thing in the morning."

"Ricky! I can't wait until tomorrow! Let's go now. Make reservations for tonight! Please!" It was well past midnight.

He walked back to the telephone and dialed 'information', asking for the number of Airways Airlines reservation number. He dialed, talked to someone, hung up and walked back to stand beside Kutzie. Looking down into her face, he told her, "I'm sorry Kutzie. They don't have a thing going out tonight to 'Frisco. We have to wait until tomorrow morning. I made the reservations for 9:00 our time, which will be 6:00 out there. We arrive at 9:45 a.m. Pacific time. Sorry. It was the best I could do."

At 6:00 a.m. Eastern time, Kutzie was dressed, and had one bag packed with two days change in it, in the event they had to stay over awhile. She went into Amber's room and sat on the side of her bed, touching her shoulder gently until Amber stirred, and opened her eyes. "What is it? What's wrong?" she asked sleepily, rubbing her eyes.

"Amber, Ricky and I are flying to San Francisco this morning. The police out there have a woman in jail who could be Crystal. I'll call you tonight, and let you know what's going on. I suppose you are going on home? I'll call you at your home."

Amber was sullen and frowning then scowling, said, "I saw that strange man hugging you. Who the hell is he anyway?"

Kutzie was taken aback because Amber was so angry even using words she had never heard her little sister use before. "Amber, sweetheart, he's a very good friend of mine. I told you he was the police officer who stopped me that Saturday morning right after I arrived in Atlanta for speeding. He didn't give me a ticket and we went out after that and I consider him a dear friend. Friends hug friends. Look at all the friends we hugged during Mom and Dad's funerals. It's just natural. I didn't dream you'd think anything about Ricky hugging me when he arrived last night."

Amber's eyes glistened with tears of relief. "I should have known that. I know that things aren't always the way they appear and I've misjudged you. Forgive me?"

Impulsively, Kutzie kissed her sister's cheek.

"Of course, sweetheart. Just remember, Ricky is a good friend, that's all."

Kutzie ran downstairs, and Ricky took her bag and they sped to the airport in his patrol car. Within the hour they were in the air heading west toward San Francisco. The flight was smooth, and could have been enjoyable if their mission had been something other than what it was.

Ricky rented a car when they landed. He asked the rental car attendant for directions to the police station, and when they arrived there the captain took them immediately to the woman's cell for identification purposes.

"Well, look, there's the stupid bitch who is so trustworthy she lets anyone take care of her brat." Kutzie's ears burned when she heard those words before she ever saw Crystal in the cell and she bristled with anger at the woman who had kidnapped her son.

"Where's my baby?" Kutzie asked through clenched teeth, when she reached Crystal's cell.

"What baby?" Crystal's lips curled, as she closed her eyes. Kutzie wanted to hit her when she looked the way she did at that moment.

"C'mon, don't give us that." Ricky told her firmly. "What have you done with Kutzie's baby boy?"

"Oh, does Kutzie have a baby boy?" Crystal jeered. "And, I suppose you're the daddy?"

"That's none of your concern. We just want to know where the baby is. Where did you leave him?" Ricky said quietly, though angrily.

"Why is she in jail, anyway?" Kutzie asked the police chief, who stood there twirling the cell keys in his hand. "What are the charges?"

"Illegal drugs. Stole a car which is why we stopped her and the drugs were found in her purse. She didn't have a baby when we caught her but she was released from jail only last month after serving time for kidnapping. Luckily, she had left the baby with a baby-sitter who eventually called us when the baby was not picked up that night. That's why we thought she may be the woman who kidnapped your baby." Kutzie was appalled! To think she had allowed such a person to tend to her baby, much less not keep an eye on her during her father's funeral. She became nauseous in the company of this loathsome woman.

"Where is my baby?" Kutzie asked impatiently her voice rising slightly, while she struggled to remain calm.

"I don't know what you're talking about, Bitch." Crystal grimaced.

"Well, we're going to have to make her talk, looks like." The police captain said in a threatening voice, as he pretended to unlock the door to Crystal's cell.

"What are you going to do?" Crystal's voice suddenly quivered with fear.

"I'm going to allow Miss Kline to come into your cell and talk to you woman to woman and face to face," he answered matter-of-factly.

Even though Kutzie was surprised that he said that her face did not show it, and Crystal screamed, "No! She'll kill me. Don't let her come in here with me!"

"Then, you'd better start talking," the officer told her, and Kutzie echoed. "He's right, Crystal and you're right, too when you say I'll kill you if I get in that cell with you. I'm ready to make you tell me the truth one way or another." As Kutzie said the words, she thought how amusing it was that Crystal believed she could do such a thing! Crystal practically made two of Kutzie, and could have sat on her, and squashed her.

"Well, hell, I guess I'll have to tell you the truth, then, stupid bitch. He died."

Kutzie almost passed out when she said that! "Oh, no!" she said, grasping Ricky's shoulder for support.

"You're lying," Ricky said, glaring at Crystal with disgust.

"Of course she is," the officer agreed. "I think we need to send her into solitary, and let her think this situation over so she can decide whether she'd rather talk or rot in the hole."

"I'll talk, I'll talk," Crystal said quickly, brushing her dull, mousy brown hair off her neck. "The baby's with a woman who lives on Texas street. That's all I know."

"And how did the baby get to the woman on Texas street?" Ricky queried, through clenched teeth.

"She was at the grocery store, and she had other kids with her. I asked her to take the baby with her because I had found it."

"Stop lying, Crystal! That story sounds as phony as a three dollar bill. Where is the baby?" Ricky queried.

She tossed her head, and her hair was so short it stood straight out like a wire brush.

"That's for me to know and you to find out." She rambled on, sticking her tongue out at Kutzie and making terrible faces at her. Kutzie felt a sense of pity for the woman for she realized she was off her rocker for sure. Ricky looked at the chief with questioning eyes, and the officer responded by making a circle with his forefinger held near one ear. Kutzie grasped Ricky's sleeve and looked up into his face trying to detect his thoughts.

"I'll get one of the women in here to question her." The officer said, barely above a whisper and walked out of the room leaving Kutzie and Ricky at Crystal's cell wondering if there was anything they could say or do to make her cooperate. In minutes he was back with a giant of a woman beside him, with a wide mouth and small eyes. Her thick eyebrows were black and bushy. Her hands were as big as any man's as she reached for the keys and opened the door of Crystal's cell.

"So you don't want to tell us where you left the child, huh?" Her voice was threatening.

Crystal fell to her knees and began crawling around the room as if she could run away from the woman. She made strange sounds, almost like an animal. Kutzie wondered if she were crazy, and the officer told her as if he had read her mind, "She's a schizophrenic, and in bad shape. We're sending her to a mental hospital for long-term treatment. She doesn't know what she's doing half the time. The decision has been made and she should be on her way by tomorrow at the latest."

Kutzie was sorry about Crystal, but nevertheless she had only feelings of hatred for the woman and hoped to never see her again. The officer kindly led Kutzie from the jail area out into the hallway and suggested she go somewhere and get some coffee and drop by a little later to find out if they learned anything else from Crystal. Kutzie nodded and the officer told her he would go get Ricky.

When Ricky came out he was furious with Crystal because, as he told Kutzie, it didn't look like she was going to tell anything. "But, let's go find a small cafe, and get a bite to eat. We need a cup of good coffee to help keep us going until that woman breaks her silence. I tell you Kutzie I never wanted to hit anyone so much in my life, as I did her, and I've never hit a woman."

"It makes me ashamed to think I'm the same species as she is." Kutzie fumed, "A human."

They were half-way down the steps leading outdoors when the officer caught them, calling, "Hey, the woman's admitted where she left your baby. C'mon back!"

Kutzie's voice caught in her throat when she tried to say something in response, because she was so very excited, and she ran back as fast as she could to Crystal's cell. As soon as she reached it Crystal saw her, and screamed, "I told you I won't tell you where the kid is until she's gone! I don't want that stuck-up bitch around me! She never liked me all the time we were in school together."

Kutzie could hardly believe what Crystal was saying and of course it wasn't true. Well, maybe it was after all. She certainly had no feelings for her now other than the pity she felt. She turned around and walked out of Crystal's sight but she didn't go back outside. She was still within ear-shot of what was being said. She heard the female officer say sharply, "Okay, tell me again where the baby is. I don't know if I understood the address right awhile ago."

And, Crystal screamed, "I left him at the library. I left him near the maps."

"But, which one? There are many libraries in town. Where were you when you left him?" The officer prodded.

Crystal yelled at the top of her voice. "I don't know! I don't know anything about this town. I was somewhere near the big bridge. I could see it as I left the library."

The officer came out of Crystal's cell slamming the door as she did so, and walked toward Kutzie standing at the end of the hall. When she approached her Kutzie stepped out so that she could see that it was she, asking, "Do you have any idea where she meant?"

The woman nodded, saying, "Yes, and we're going to send someone right over. Where will you be waiting in the meantime?"

Kutzie looked at Ricky, waiting to see if he had an answer. He thought about it briefly, then answered, "We'll be right over there in that little coffee shop. Just call us there or have someone walk down to get us. We're mighty anxious to get that boy."

Oh no! I think he's going to try to figure up the date again of Chase's birth, and, back to the night when we made love! But, there's a full month's difference. He can't possibly know that Chase was an 'eight-month baby'.

They strolled across to the little greasy-spoon coffee shop, and when they were seated in one of the booths, Kutzie put a hand to her forehead and sighing, said, "Ricky, I can't for the life of me believe I left my baby with a woman who is as crazy as a loon, evidently."

Reaching across the booth to take her hands in his, he smiled, "How could you know? Isn't she an old school chum whom you've known practically all your life? You had no way of knowing she's gone off the deep end for whatever reason, and it would be natural to accept her offer of generosity to baby-sit while you were grieving at your dad's funeral. By the way, I don't remember if I ever offered my condolences to you and your sister? I am so sorry you've lost both your parents, and especially so close together like that!"

Kutzie had filled him in on most of the sordid details that morning, regarding her mom's illness and eventual death, how her father had endured the trials of her illness while attempting to take care of her and himself for as long as he could. She mentioned that she had not realized her father was as ill as he must have been, although Amber had called several times during the past year to tell her again and again that he was not well. She wondered if perhaps he had grieved himself to death for allowing a nursing home to take over the responsibilities that he considered to be his own? Ricky assured her she had no reason to feel guilty, for how could she know that he was as tired as he was? He added that it sounded to him as if Richard was exhausted from trials he had endured, and that his heart just stopped to rest. Kutzie felt a little more comforted. About then the owner of the establishment walked to their table, asking "Are you Kutzie Kline?"

"Yes?" her voice was so quiet it was barely audible as she looked up at him with wonder.

"Someone on the phone said to tell you they're ready for you. I guess you know what that means?"

"Yes, I know, thank you." She smiled and wiping her mouth she stood up, and headed for the door. Ricky fumbled in his pocket for his wallet and tip money, paid the check and ran to catch up with her.

As she ran inside the station, he took her arms and said "Kutzie, I'm here with you. Don't just run off like that and leave me." She didn't care that his voice was stern, she went on inside, and with eyes glistening with the tears that were forming, said, "I'm sorry, Ricky. I just can't wait to get my baby son back. I'm very frightened."

"He'll be okay and we'll be headed home in a little while." His face was dark, and angry.

She slowed her pace and whispered, "I was just thinking, I've always longed to see San Francisco and this experience has left such a bad taste in my mouth, I never want to return!"

"You'll feel differently when everything's calmed down and back to normal again. We'll be back one day to see the city . . . the real San Francisco. This isn't it by a long-shot!"

The jailer was standing beside the door as they walked in, and he handed Ricky a piece of paper with an address on it. "The Sergeant is on the phone now talking to someone about your baby, who, it seems, was left on a park bench and was picked up by the animal shelter patrol wagon. He's been taken to another precinct," the elderly, gray-haired may explained. "That is where you'll be taken to."

"The animal control wagon picked him up on a park bench?" Kutzie was visibly shaken. "My god, Ricky, anything could have happened to him!" Kutzie cried. Ricky agreed.

The precinct was not too far from where they were, but it seemed like a hundred miles to Kutzie, and she counted the minutes as hours on the drive over. A woman officer was holding Chase when they walked in, and Kutzie took the baby from her arms, and kissed him all over his face and neck and hands, crying so hard the tears fogged her vision. It was a sight to behold as the entire roomful of people stopped what they had been doing to witness the moving scene. Ricky too, seemed to have tears in his eyes Kutzie noticed. Kutzie examined every inch of the baby searching for a bruise or any tell-tale marks of abuse and finding none, she hugged the baby close to her body and nestled his head in her arms.

The flight home from San Francisco was much happier than the one they had made earlier coming in from Charlotte. Kutzie had called Amber from the airport to let her know what had gone on and Amber asked that they please hurry back home, as she and Randy had worried themselves sick over what may have happened to the baby.

That evening after supper and a celebration, and after Amber and Randy had gone home and the baby was in bed for the night, Kutzie and Ricky sat on the front porch as the cool breezes blew, and talked. Kutzie had a hunch that Ricky was pressing hard for details regarding her pregnancy and the baby's birth because he suspected that he was the father. She tried hard not to give away the secret that hers was an eight-month pregnancy.

After awhile, Ricky told her in a sneering tone of voice that surprised Kutzie, that he might as well head west and go on to Atlanta. She wondered why he sounded so flippant but asked sweetly, "Won't it be too hard on you to make the trip as tired as you must be?"

"I'm not tired. Besides, I have things to do once I get back home and it doesn't matter how long I'm on the road or how late it is when I get there. I'm off work until tomorrow night."

He stood up to leave and when Kutzie rose he took her in his arms, and kissed her hard and furious on the lips, so hard that the pressure actually pained her. "Ouch!" she cried.

"Oh, I'm sorry. Well, s'long, Sweets. I'll be back in a few days so the baby and I can test our blood together. All right?"

Chapter Nine

The Showdown

She gasped. This was a shock! Was he serious? He hadn't mentioned anything whatsoever about that although it had to be as she suspected that he thought he was Chase's father. He hadn't even hinted however that he may be suspicious enough to have their blood compared, or if he had said anything along those lines, she was not aware of it at that time. She had dismissed any reasons for those questions he had asked, because she thought he was simply interested in how she had fared through the pregnancy.

She finally managed to ask, "Why? What do you want to do that for?"

"I think he's mine. Look at the eyes. He looks exactly like a baby picture of me that's in the family album."

She scoffed. "All babies look alike. I look at baby pictures of relatives, and they all look the same."

His eyebrows were knitted together as he answered, "I doubt that it's that way in this case. He's the spitting image of me in an old photo that I told you I have. I'll be back, little gal, and if he's mine we should get married. If he isn't mine then you have nothing to worry about, right?" She said nothing.

She watched him, still speechless, as he got into his patrol car, and drove away.

For hours she sat outside thinking. The intercom to the baby's room revealed that the baby was sleeping, and occasionally stirring in his crib, as she sat wondering what it would be like married to Ricky, and loving Bill. She needed to write to Bill to answer his letter! She had to talk to him! She missed him so much she ached inside and knew she could not stay away from his as she had thought she would.

She finally went upstairs, and to bed.

Morning found her and the baby effervescent and happy to be together again. Kutzie played with him, tickling his belly and blowing on it, as she bathed him, making him smile.

Amber called to see how things were going and Kutzie told her she thought she would go to Atlanta for awhile and check on things and would probably be back to see her in a week or two. Amber came over on her lunch hour to see little Chase and to tell them 'bye for the time being.

It was around noon when Kutzie pulled into the massive, steel gates to the mansion, elated to be home. She was going to call Bill as soon as she could get to the telephone! That, she had decided already!

However, the first thing she did upon arriving was to call all the hired help to ask them to return to work the next day. Next she called Elite. When Bill answered the phone she was excited to hear his voice. "Bill? How are you?" she asked, her voice choking in her throat.

"Kutzie? Where are you, sweetheart? My God, I can't believe it's you! I've been going out of my mind with worry because no one has heard from you in so long. Did you receive my letter?"

"Yes, but I'm home. Would you like to come over?"

"Home? The mansion, you mean?"

"Of course."

"Yes! I'll be over as soon as I get off work. In fact if I can get Leona to let me go a little earlier I will. I can't wait to see you!"

She was so ecstatic, she held Chase close to her and danced through the house with him, humming and laughing and singing. She watched the clock all afternoon.

When the household staff arrived, they were all happy to see her back, and lavished much attention on her and the baby. Kutzie felt that at long last they cared for and respected her as much as they did the Hunt family. She told the nanny she was expecting an important guest after five that evening, and that she would like her to bring the baby in shortly after six. She could hardly contain herself as it neared five o'clock. She had been very scrupulous about the way she dressed for him, wanting to look her very best for Bill.

Apparently, she succeeded in pleasing him for he gathered her in his arms as soon as she answered the door herself, when the gate telephone rang, and then the doorbell.

She fell into his arms calling his name over and over, as they kissed each other hungrily, and clung to one another as though they would never let go. They snuggled in each other's arms, seeing no need for words and they sat together side by side on the couch, staring into each other's eyes, drinking in each other's every facial feature, and smiling dreamily.

"I love you." Bill whispered kissing the tip of her nose.

"I love you, too," she whispered back.

"I don't know if I ever told you how sorry I was regarding Rusty's death," he whispered as he kissed her forehead. "I was at the funeral, you remember and it seemed like every time I called your house after that, you were never in. And, then, you left to go to Charlotte, and no one heard from you after that, except we knew about your parents' untimely death. When I wrote you that letter and you didn't answer, I was frantic with worry. I thought you loved me once but I was worried that you were simply going to forget you ever knew me."

She looked at him a moment, scanning his face as her eyes filled with tears, and answered honestly, "I was going to try, Bill, because I didn't want you to hate me. I left and stayed gone because I was pregnant. I wanted to keep it from you because I knew you would think I was a terrible person."

He was startled, and a look of grim surprise crossed the face she considered beloved, and finally he asked, "You were pregnant? You have a baby?"

She nodded, hoping he wouldn't ask too many questions. She had vowed to never lie to him again, no matter what. If she were to tell him it was Rusty's baby, and the blood tests proved he belonged to Ricky, how would she explain that? It was hard enough to admit to him that she had slept with Rusty when they were engaged, much less admit she had slept with Ricky as well, after she became engaged to Rusty.

"Where is the baby? Is it a boy or a girl?" Bill asked.

"A boy. His name is Chase. He's upstairs in the nursery. The nanny's going to bring him down in a few minutes."

He was speechless. He said nothing for a full minute just sat staring into her eyes with a far-away look in his own, seemingly searching her face for whatever . . . a clue for why she did such a thing?

"Now what?" he asked quietly.

"What do you mean, 'now what?' " she asked.

"Do you have any plans of any kind? Rusty's dead. Are you going to keep the baby and raise him alone?"

"What do you suggest?" she asked so quietly it was barely audible. There had never been a question in her mind about whether or not she would keep the baby.

"I think you can't raise him alone. I think he needs a daddy. I think you need a husband. I think you need me." He was practically laughing by the time he finished making suggestions.

Her mouth dropped open, and she gasped, then grabbed him around the neck, and squealed, "Oh, Bill! Darling! Darling! Is this a proposal?"

"You know it is. You know I've told you all along I was waiting for you to decide when you were ready to marry if you wanted me. I feel like you're ready now."

"You name the date and I'll be ready. Do you want to plan a real wedding or would you rather elope? Whatever you decide is fine with me."

They had much to talk about the rest of the evening. When the nanny brought Chase in and Kutzie introduced him, Bill smiled with obvious approval. Bill clued her in on all that had been going on at Elite, and she told him how her father had died. She mentioned that the baby had been taken away by her friend, but did not call it a kidnapping. In fact, she simply had not told him all the details, and let it hang in the balance as though it had been no big deal at all. If he wondered where her friend had taken the baby, he didn't ask.

When he left late in the evening, neither of them were ready to part. He promised to call and would see her the next day after work, for sure. He had been gone less than an hour when Ricky called surprising her because it was as late as it was. "Well, I thought I'd find you here in town since I wasn't able to reach you in Charlotte. You must've left Charlotte when I did? Couldn't bear it without me, huh?"

"I did leave there about an hour or so later. It was a sudden decision but I saw no reason to stay since no one lived in the house any more, and I have this house here with all my things in it."

"Well, I need to know Chase's blood-type tonight. Do you know what it is?"

"No. Why?"

"Because I know he belongs to me. I have O-negative blood. What is yours?"

"O-positive."

"Wonder what Rusty's was? Do you know?"

"Yes." And, said no more than that. It was none of his business.

She knew because once in conversation, Lana had mentioned that Rusty's Type-B blood was rare, and at the time of his birth, he had complications due to her blood-type of positive, and Charles' blood-type of negative, and had to have a blood transfusion or something. She had no real interest in the subject at the time, and had allowed it to go in one ear and out the other. Perhaps she should contact Lana and tell her of the baby's arrival and ask her again about Rusty's blood type, and then call the hospital to ask about Chase's type.

There had been messages on the machine from Lana when she returned home from Charlotte, and she planned to call later and talk with her and Charles.

"I've made an appointment for tomorrow morning at 9:00 for us to go in and get the blood tests so we'll know." She heard Ricky say, interrupting her thoughts.

She didn't know what to say and so was silent for a moment then she said, "Ricky, the baby belongs to Rusty."

"You don't know that and I don't know that, so we'll find out for sure, rather than argue about it. I talked to the doctor and was told that Chase could have been early. Happens all the time. Anyway, I'll pick you up at 8:30 tomorrow morning, and you be ready, okay?"

When he hung up without waiting for an answer, she was shaken. He was rude and demanding the way he talked, and then hung up so quickly the way he did, but why was he pursuing this anyway? What did it matter if the baby belonged to him? She wasn't asking for child-support or anything, and he could see the baby at any time.

The next day she called the Hunt's residence in Dallas, but they were not there. She knew they were going to return to Greece when they left that last time after Rusty's funeral, and had said they would be home in June. That was only two-and-a-half weeks away, and she had no idea how to contact them, since Lana had not left a message when she called, nor had she written at all. Chris had been the one who called his parents in Greece when Rusty died. She decided to call Chris and Andrea, and ask if they would notify Lana, and have her call her again at the mansion. She reached their answering machine and left a message.

Leona called early, about 7:30 just to ask how she was, and then Bill. She and Leona talked only a couple of minutes, and, she and Bill cooed together for almost a half-hour. She considered telling him about Ricky, and what he was saying about Chase but that would be another worry on Bill's shoulders, and he didn't need that she decided. Neither did she.

She asked the nanny to dress Chase to go out, while she ate a quick bite of cereal, and then dressed in a pair of red-and-white floral slacks, and a loose, white cotton sweater. She no longer wore anything too tight across her milk-filled bosom.

Ricky was there promptly at 8:30, and when she released the gate for him, he pulled in and stopped in the circular drive and blew the horn, while he sat in the car. She was surprised at his indifference. He had always been the perfect gentleman and so helpful coming to her rescue when Junior was bothering her, and when Chase was kidnapped a couple of days ago.

Now, he was grim and tight-lipped and very unfriendly when she got in beside him. She smiled, and said "Good morning," but he simply grunted, and said nothing. He pulled back the blanket from Chase's head, and looked down at the sleeping baby, still not saying anything. He simply looked angry.

He parked in the parking lot of the doctor's office, and took Chase from her, and carried the baby inside himself. The doctor greeted them as he had stepped into the waiting room briefly talking to a patient that he had seen already. He told them to have a seat, and that someone would be with them shortly. Kutzie felt strange about being there, and a sense of foreboding made her very uncomfortable.

* * *

As they drove away from the doctor's office, Ricky tossed the piece of paper into Kutzie's lap, and asked, curtly, "Is there any place in particular you'd like to get married?"

"What?" she asked, taken aback by his tone of voice, besides the assumption that they were going to get married, simply because the doctor had said the baby definitely belonged to him.

"Where are we going to get married? We need to make the baby something other than a bastard."

"A BASTARD? How dare you? How can you say such a thing about that poor little baby?"

"That's exactly what he is, isn't he?" Ricky asked, and his whole countenance had changed from the sweet, good-looking young man she had admired during the past thirteen months, to an ugly contemptible individual who reminded her of that day last year when he had stopped her for speeding. She was bristling, ready to erupt at any time because of his attitude. She didn't know this person!

"I don't want to get married." She stated the fact simply, and sternly.

"Well, fine. But, how are we going to split the baby? Do you think you're going to keep him?"

"What are you talking about?" she felt her face redden as the anger welled up inside her.

"He's my child, and I want him. I want him full-time, not just on week-ends, or that kind of shit."

"I don't know that you're going to see him any time, not with that attitude, anyway," she scowled.

"Don't threaten me and make me do something you'll regret later," he raged. "For example, what kind of mother are you when you didn't even know who the baby belonged to? He could have been Junior's for all you knew! Besides, you certainly didn't care who you left him with, did you? You allowed that crazy woman to baby-sit him?"

"Oh, you make me sick!" she fumed. "You know that's not the way it happened at all."

"How do I know it isn't? Tell me! Did you know for sure who the baby belonged to? You told me Rusty, but you said that simply because you were engaged to marry the guy because he was wealthy, and you wanted all you could get out of him."

"Ricky! I can't believe you're saying these things to me! I thought you cared for me!"

"I thought I did, too, until I found out that you've been whoring around with every Tom, Dick and Harry in this town. You had me fooled, sister, that's all I can say."

"But you know better than that. You know things can happen, you said so. And that's what it was. Like the night you and I slipped up, and it happened the same way with Rusty."

"Sure, the night you and I slipped up. You had on a flimsy pair of pajamas you were running around in before me, and those other policemen. What kind of standards did that show? Absolutely no morals at all."

"Now, I see why your first wife left you for her boss." she said, without thinking. His hand lashed out across her face, and the force of the slap caused pain that penetrated through her head. Stunned, she thought of clawing his eyes out, but was suddenly afraid of this monster she didn't know!

Little Chase was asleep in his car-bed on the back seat and she looked back at his cherub little innocent face wondering how he could look like such an angel yet have this man up here at the wheel claiming to be his father. If she started a physical fight, Ricky may have an accident, and Chase may be hurt. She could not handle that!

"Don't EVER say anything like that again, do you understand?" he hissed, angrily.

"You can go to hell, Ricky Larson, for all I care." she lashed out, and moved toward the door. She wanted him to think she may jump out though she wouldn't and leave her baby. When he parked in front of her house she grabbed Chase and scampered to get out of this madman's car. He warned her in a threatening voice, "Don't get any ideas about leaving Atlanta with my son. You can't get away from me and should you try, I'll go to court and take him away from you. Just remember, judges don't care for unfit mothers."

She ran into the house, shaking, and wishing for someone to talk to. How she needed her parents now! There was absolutely no one she could turn to! Bill? No! He'd most assuredly hate her if he knew about Rick.

But, she had to tell him! She could not keep it from him, especially now that Ricky was threatening her. She planned how she would say it. She said the words aloud to her mirror, practicing on what would sound best. Nothing sounded right! It would come out of her mouth as though she were an unfit mother just as Ricky had accused her. She sat down on the chaise in her bedroom and thought about everything, then went into the nursery and picked up Chase. Later, she lay across her bed with Chase lying beside her, and cuddled him close and nuzzling her head against him she cried her eyes out. When Bill called on the telephone, she quickly straightened up and attempted to get control of her emotions before she fell apart.

She wasn't sure how much more she could take! Every day a new problem seemed to crop up to break her heart and she had to stay strong.

Bill certainly must have detected the anguish in her voice, because he asked, "Is something wrong, Honey? What's going on?"

That was all it took! She began to weep as though she would never stop! The sobs were raspy, and she was unable to answer. She heard him say, "I'll be right there," And, the phone went dead.

At that precise hour it was not difficult to sob out the entire shameful story when he arrived, and he held her in his arms while she sobbed out the story. He bristled with rage when she mentioned that Ricky had slapped her. "He actually slapped you on the face?" he asked, and his face reddened with anger which was unusual for a man with such control over his emotions as Bill Davis had always had in the past.

She nodded.

"Well, if I ever see that low-down, good-for-nothing idiot face to face, I'll give him a dose of his own medicine," he stormed. Then, softly, he whispered, "I think Ricky has answered our question for us. You know, we couldn't decide on whether or not to have a big wedding, or to elope. What say we elope? Now! We can drive over to Jenson County, and get our license and blood tests, and get married there tomorrow. Okay?"

She nodded, and said she would like to call her sister, and tell her. He laughed because of her enthusiasm and sat beside her with an arm around her shoulder while she broke the news to Amber, who seemed somewhat bewildered by the men in Kutzie's life.

* * *

They found a Justice-of-the-Peace after the results of their blood tests came back, and the man's wife was their only witness to the wedding ceremony. When they came out of the house as man and wife, both were walking on air. She was now Mrs. Bill Davis, and she loved the sound of the name, as well as the man!

They returned to the mansion, and hurried upstairs to the nursery to get Chase. Bill carried the baby downstairs, and held him while they sat in the den discussing future plans, as well as how they would handle Ricky whenever he called.

Kutzie gave the nanny the night off because Bill said he would welcome the opportunity to get better acquainted with 'his son'. Kutzie felt warm and touched by his incredible love.

When Ricky did call, neither of them expected the reaction upon his learning that she had already married someone else. He literally exploded with rage! He ranted and raved, and began accusing her of trying to steal his son away from him, and swore he was going to take Chase away from her. He threatened Bill, telling him if he caught him outside he would deal with him in the way he deserved.

When they hung up, Bill turned to Kutzie, and with a questioning look across his face, he said, "There's something fishy about that guy." He suddenly snapped his fingers, and Kutzie almost saw the light come on in his head. "Kutzie, do you know the doctor who did the blood tests?" She shook her head. "He must be Ricky's doctor. I had never heard of him, myself."

"Do you have his name and address?"

"I remember where the office is located. I saw the name of the doctor on the door, but I can't remember what it was."

"Let's go over there. I have a sneaking suspicion that Ricky is pulling the wool over your eyes. He's too upset about your marrying me, and I think he doesn't care beans about the baby. It's simply his way of getting you for himself."

She shook his head. "I doubt it, Bill. I don't think he even likes me. He was rude and as I told you, he slapped me. In general, he showed no feelings of respect for me whatsoever. He called me a tramp."

"That's because he's a creep, that's all. He may not respect any woman, for his own unknown reasons." And, when she heard that, Kutzie remembered what Ricky had told her about his wife leaving him for her boss when she went to work at the advertising agency.

"I'd like to have a talk with that doctor." Bill continued.

Kutzie grabbed her handbag, and Chase's diaper bag, and holding Bill's hand with one hand, and Chase in the other, and the diaper bag hanging on Bill's shoulder, they ran outside and scampered into Bill's Lexus, and headed toward the doctor's office.

"What do you think Ricky has done?" Kutzie inquired, not even able to imagine what Bill had in mind.

"I think he's paid a doctor to say the baby has his blood type. I want to see if I can find out what type of blood Ricky has, and then we'll take the baby to be tested somewhere else."

"Do you think the doctor is going to tell you that? I don't thinks so, Bill, darling. You're going to have to come up with something else."

He slowed the car, and glanced soberly into her green eyes, and with a crooked smile he nodded his head in agreement. "Of course. Hey! I just thought! I have a good friend who works at the Court House. I wonder if he can find out for us what Ricky's blood type is? They have to have information like that on hand, in the event an officer is injured. Ya think?"

She nodded, excited that they may be able to put something over on Ricky once and for all.

Bill headed toward downtown, and toward the City Courthouse. They walked in together, and studied the director of services, and went up to the second floor. There, he saw his old friend, Ken Loden, and introduced him to his wife, Kutzie. Anyone who may have been looking on, could have detected the admiration in Ken's eyes as he looked Kutzie over, however surreptitiously he may have tried to be. They went into Ken's private office, and he had his secretary bring coffee. When Bill told him all the story, he agreed with Bill that it sounded fishy to him, too, about the way Ricky had been in such a hurry to get married, and had thrown such a tantrum when he learned she had married Bill.

"Still, you can't blame the guy for getting upset when he thought he was going to marry a beautiful lady, such as Kutzie, only to find out hours later, that the lady has already married someone else." He chuckled low, and Bill agreed, while Kutzie simply smiled modestly. "Let me see what I can find out for you." Ken suggested. "Give me the name and address of the doctor, and I'll get started on checking him out, as well as finding out Ricky's blood type."

"I can't remember the doctor." Kutzie's eyebrows arched in a furrow. "Only the location."

"That'll do." Ken assured her. "Give me the address."

As Bill and Kutzie drove back to the mansion, both were ecstatic. Bill felt confident in his original thought that Ricky was trying to pull the wool over Kutzie's eyes and would be thwarted in his attempt to do it.

That night when they had gone to bed they consummated their marriage in true, genuine love. Neither had known such deep feelings of commitment in all their lives, and even though Kutzie's world was in turmoil, she felt at peace lying in Bill's strong arms, listening to his heart beat after he had fallen asleep. She sighed with the comfortable feeling that Bill could fix anything and once she almost lost that security in her life because of her coyness.

At eight the next morning the telephone rang, rousing Kutzie from a deep sleep. She reached across her pillow feeling for Bill, and awoke with a start, when she realized he was not beside her. Sleepily, she answered the phone. It was Lana! "Morning, Kutzie, dear. Did I wake you? I'm sorry."

"Mother!" Kutzie sat straight up in the bed, and the name popped out of her mouth before she realized it. "Where in the world are you?"

"We're back in Dallas. Charles has a convention to attend in Atlanta next week and we hoped to drop by and visit you, to see how you're doing. Are you free Tuesday?"

Kutzie wondered how much to tell her on the telephone so she simply said, "Yes, of course I am, and I can't wait to see you and Dad." 'Mother and Dad' had not been easy to say before, but she truly felt that they were her family, in spite of the fact she had not spent a lot of time with them, but long enough to learn to love them.

When Kutzie's other line rang, the gracious Lana said, "Well, you have another call so I'll go for now, but I'll call you before we leave here next week. And, Kutzie, we're anxious to see you, too. We haven't meant to neglect you, it's just the way we are."

Kutzie assured her she understood, and they hung up so Kutzie could answer the other line. It was Bill with a smile in his voice, "Good morning, sweetheart, did I wake you?"

"Bill, where are you, stinker? Did you go to the office? I though we were going to have a few days together. A honeymoon?" Actually she was only teasing because they had talked the night before about a honeymoon during the July 4th weekend when Amber and Randy could come to Atlanta to stay with Chase. Kutzie felt more comfortable about leaving him with Amber, rather than with Tammi the nanny, because with Tammi it was simply her job and Amber had been asking to keep him a few days so they could bond. She had a lot of love for the baby and her husband, Randy had seen very little of the then three-week-old Chase at the time Kutzie left Charlotte.

"I didn't want to leave you, but I felt I should, little darling." Bill answered. "I wasn't sure if I should tell anyone here at the office that we had slipped off and got married, or if you wanted to be the one to break the news to the world?"

"It doesn't matter," she giggled. "I want to shout it to the housetops."

"So do I," he answered. "I love you, Kutzie."

"I love you, too, Mister Davis."

The other line rang, and it was Ken. She told him she was on the other line talking to Bill at the office, and he said he would call him there, and they hung up.

She told Bill, "That was Ken. He's going to call you."

"Great! Maybe he has some good news for us? I'll let you go now, darling, and I'll call you again in a little while. Kiss Chase for me."

She smiled at his thoughtfulness as she lay the phone in its cradle. It was unusual that he had so much love for her baby already, when he had seen him only twice, and briefly at that. She knew that he was sincere, and that he was going to make a wonderful father.

Quickly, she took a warm shower and donned a white jumpsuit, and a pair of white sandals. She tied her hair back in a pony-tail with a white ribbon. She rang for Tammi, the nanny, to get Chase dressed to go out.

The phone rang. It was Bill. "Kutzie, Ken says the doctor over there is under investigation for fraudulent blood tests. Was the doctor Ricky saw named 'Shah'?"

"Yes, that's it," she answered quickly. "That was the name on the door. Abdul Shah."

"Well, he says they hope to have something to tell us later on today so when he calls back, I'll call you. Leona said to tell you 'hello'. Do they know about Chase? I'm assuming they don't, since I didn't know he existed myself until I came over, and you surprised me with the news."

"No. I haven't told them."

"Well, let's just play that by ear, and see what happens. For the life of me, I can't see how you hid a pregnancy from everyone. You had to have a tummy."

"Only during the last month, and no one saw me during that time. I wasn't eating very much and that kept me from showing, I guess, but when I started eating right in order to get some weight on the baby then I started looking pregnant."

"You stinker you. You completely amaze me some times." he chuckled. "That's why I love you so much."

"Bill, I'm going to take the baby, and go over to Hubbard's, and see how things are going. I need to buy a couple of things while I'm out. Want to go to lunch? I can drive by and pick you up around 11:30 if that's a good time."

"It sounds like a perfect time, honey. Okay then. Pick me up out front?"

She was proud as she showed off the baby to certain ones at Hubbard's who had known Rusty well and they all said, without exception, that they could see the resemblance. Kutzie was elated to hear that because she could see more and more that he resembled Rusty and she saw nothing that denoted that he could belong to Ricky.

As she shopped in the Infants Department, she thought back on how she had hoped only a year ago to be able to one day be able to shop for an item in Hubbard's, and now it belonged to her, lock, stock and barrel. She had to pinch herself at times to realize that fact. Bill was waiting for her when she stopped in front of Elite at 11:25. When he jumped in and kissed her, she smiled, "Goodness, I was prepared to have to wait on you but you were already outside waiting on us?"

"I have wonderful news, baby. The doctor admitted he signed that fraudulent document for Ricky, because Ricky paid him $500 to do so. The baby really doesn't belong to Ricky, because the baby has Type B blood, and the doctor admitted Ricky could not be the father, because his is A-negative. Not only that, Ricky and the doctor are involved in other schemes and both have been arrested and are on their way to jail as we speak."

So, he even lied about his blood-type!

Kutzie was overjoyed to hear that! "Thank God," she

tittered happily. "That eliminates a lot of unmerited problems from ol' Ricky, doesn't it?"

"Honey, how did you ever get mixed up with people like Ricky, and Junior anyway?"

"Just lucky, I guess," she joked.

"I've wondered why Junior was stalking you, and how he was able to get into the gates that night when he came to the mansion when the attacks took place?"

"The butler, Rodney, mentioned to me not long ago that when the gardener left for the day he forgot to close the gates securely, and Junior must have been hanging around after following us there, and he got in before it was discovered. And, one day as I was thinking about things, I recalled that the first day I came into town, and was looking for Elite, that red pickup of Junior's was behind me for several blocks. That had to be Junior! He must have seen me when I was stopped at a red light or something, and followed me, thinking I was that judge who sent him to prison over ten years ago. I think he probably followed you and me either that day or on another day, and that's how he knew where I lived. He must have been following me just about everywhere, and followed me even to Studebaker's that night."

"But, I wonder how he dropped a knock-out pill in my drink that night without us seeing him? He had to be the one who did that!" Bill grimaced.

"I have no idea how," she admitted. "Perhaps we were so engrossed with each other, we didn't pay any attention. But, since you had never seen him before, you wouldn't have paid any attention to him if he'd just passed by. I can see how he could get by with something like that, now that I think about it."

They went to The Swan Coach House for lunch, and when other diners came by to tell them what a beautiful baby they had Bill beamed as much as Kutzie did, and thanked them sincerely for the compliment.

Kutzie had considered going in to see her friends at Elite when Bill returned from lunch, but she was too exhilarated with the good news Bill had brought, and didn't want to be deflated yet, and drove on home to her comfortable home to relax.

Lana called again that afternoon. "Kutzie, dear, I'm sorry to have to tell you, but Charles and I are not going to be in Atlanta after all this next week. We've decided to take a trip to Japan and stay a year or so. I really would love to see you before we go but there's not going to be enough time. I'll try to write often, although I'm not a very good letter-writer. I'll call you when we return to the states if not before, okay?"

At first, Kutzie was disappointed but when she thought about it, she wasn't sure if their being there next week would have been the right time or not. She would one day tell them they had a grandson but for now, she determined they were not ready for that kind of news.

Perhaps they would drop by to see her one day, and get acquainted with Chase, and meet his adoptive father, Bill, the sweetest person in the entire world! What a wonderful life!

I'm going to call Amber right now, and tell her what a perfect ending this story has, even though she doesn't know all that's been going on. Thank God everything's at last coming up roses!

THE END

About the Author

Jeannette Grindele has written stories for as long as she can remember. Even while attending elementary school, she used to write fictitious biographies of her schoolmates, draw their photo and attach it to their story, and sell it to them for a nickel or dime.

She bought her first typewriter in 1980 in order to make her novels look more professional (she had handwritten them before), but her husband poked fun at her desire to write, and so she hid them back before they were finished. She claims to have a zillion stories in her head, both fiction and nonfiction, begging to be released on paper.

Her children have encouraged her along the way to pursue her love of writing, and to publish her work, not stash it away on a shelf in the closet. All of her five children are married, and when she was widowed in 1990, writing became her source of strength and her computer her companion, and she now devotes every spare moment to her writing.

Watch for her novels in the future. She plans to publish a children's book next year.